*"Don't think, Zoe," Stephen whispered.
"Just do what comes naturally."*

It seemed that attacking this sexy man was what Zoe found natural. Not that he was complaining. Within minutes, she was lying on top of him on the couch, holding him captive. His hands had slid to her hips, cradling her against his groin. Good Lord, was that his erection?

"Please," he rasped against her cheek. "Please say we can partner. We can teach each other so much."

Why not? She was open to wandering in the sexual wilds for a while with this man. And after all, a Tantric orgasm was supposed to be the height of physical ecstasy.

Not trusting her voice, she nodded. He smiled, but then his eyes darkened and his jaw became granite. All of a sudden Zoe realized that Stephen wasn't just any man. He was a Tantric master. She felt his power vibrate in the air between them. It was energy, charged enough to make every cell in her body tingle. She was on fire!

"Is it always like this?" she gasped, trying to regain some control.

He chuckled softly. "Sweet Zoe, it has only begun...."

Blaze

Dear Reader,

My daughter had her first job this summer. She worked the morning shift at Panera Bread, beginning at 4:30 a.m. This was very hard for her, especially since come September, she went to school after her shift. In fact, it was so hard that she decided to quit. Thankfully, she wasn't paying her tuition, so she could afford that luxury.

But what if she couldn't? I thought about all the working students in the world, sweating through minimum-wage jobs to pay for their education, all in the name of a better tomorrow. I raise my latte to all of you! And here's an extra dollar in the tip jar.

Zoe Lewis's situation in this story was inspired by my daughter's summer job experience. Having made a few bad choices in her life, Zoe is now intent on that better tomorrow, but she has to get through school first. The weight of all the work she has to do just beats her down until everything is too hard. The last thing on her mind is a man. Where would she find the time?

But like all those struggling students, Zoe deserves an amazing future. She deserves a man and a career and most especially love. And like an awesome surprise in the tip jar, her love comes in a very unusual package!

Happy reading,

Jade
jade@jadeleeauthor.com

Jade Lee

GETTING PHYSICAL

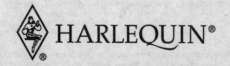

TORONTO • NEW YORK • LONDON
AMSTERDAM • PARIS • SYDNEY • HAMBURG
STOCKHOLM • ATHENS • TOKYO • MILAN • MADRID
PRAGUE • WARSAW • BUDAPEST • AUCKLAND

Recycling programs
for this product may
not exist in your area.

ISBN-13: 978-0-373-79493-5

GETTING PHYSICAL

www.eHarlequin.com

Printed in U.S.A.

ABOUT THE AUTHOR

A *USA TODAY* bestselling author, Jade Lee has made her mark with sizzling romances. She adores unique settings, dark characters and erotic, exotic love. And if she throws in a dragon or a tigress here and there, it's only in the name of fun! An author of more than thirty novels, she loves the fabulousness that is Harlequin Blaze! She calls them her sexy treat and hopes you find them equally delicious. Jade loves hearing from readers. Visit her at www.jadeleeauthor.com or e-mail her at jade@jadeleeauthor.com.

Books by Jade Lee
HARLEQUIN BLAZE
374—THE TAO OF SEX
449—THE CONCUBINE

Don't miss any of our special offers. Write to us at the following address for information on our newest releases.

Harlequin Reader Service
U.S.: 3010 Walden Ave., P.O. Box 1325, Buffalo, NY 14269
Canadian: P.O. Box 609, Fort Erie, Ont. L2A 5X3

_1_

STEPHEN CHU banged his fist heavily against the apartment door. After almost two days of travel from Hong Kong, he was dropping with fatigue. He'd already passed through three Herculean trials. Impatience—an endless wait for the first flight out of Hong Kong. Poverty—expensive in-flight phone calls to rescue his father's business legacy. And then bureaucracy—that god-awful line at Customs. He would not be stopped now by a locked door. He wouldn't. He banged again.

"He's not there," said a voice behind him.

Stephen spun around, his fist tensing around the handle of his garment bag. The bag was unwieldy, but could still be used to buy time in a fight. Then he blinked, his brain catching up to reality. The voice had been female and friendly. And coming from farther down the hall.

A blond waif emerged from the shadows, a backpack on her shoulders. She looked about sixteen years old and was staring at him with that wide-eyed awe that was more nuisance than flattery.

He relaxed his grip on the bag and resorted to his second line of defense: charm. "I'm sorry, I didn't see you there. You say Mr. Gao isn't at home?"

She dropped her backpack on the ground and slid to the floor. "He's late. Pull up a chair. We can wait together."

He blinked and looked up and down the hall. There wasn't a chair in sight.

She snorted. "It was a joke. Sit on the garment bag if the floor's too gross for you." She watched him, humor dancing in her blue eyes as she waited for his decision.

He looked at the floor. In truth, it was clean—about a two-star-hotel quality. He'd stayed in much worse. But he very much feared that if he sat, he'd never stand up again. "Actually, I'm not looking for Mr. Gao, but Miss Tracy Williams. Do you know where she might be?"

"She's with Nathan, of course."

The waif smiled, and in that instant Stephen noticed two things. First, she was older than he'd thought. There was a seriousness in her eyes even though the rest of her face dimpled with humor. It didn't make sense, but when she smiled, her eyes remained sad, the kind of sadness that came only from experience. And second, he saw that she was very beautiful. How had he missed that before?

Meanwhile, the girl continued to chat about Nathan and Tracy. "They're still in that newly engaged stage where they're inseparable."

"Yes, they are good friends. That's why I'm here—" His mind lurched. Fatigue was making it too damn slow. "Did you say engaged?"

"Yup. Tracy and Nathan are going to be married. Apparently it happened right in the middle of a drug bust or something. The cops were after someone else on a different floor. There was some shooting, but everyone is fine. I heard about it from 2B, who heard it from…" Her voice trailed away. "But you don't really care about that, do you? So why do you want Tracy?"

"She is… She was to be…" He swallowed, unsettled

not by the information but by an inability to think. "Jet lag," he groused. "Engaged? To Nathan? But why?"

The waif released another unladylike snort. "Because they're in love? That is the usual reason."

He heard bitterness in her voice and he silently echoed it. His parents had been in "love" once, too, or so he was told. It wasn't real, it wasn't even pretty, or it hadn't been during his very lonely childhood. He wondered if love—or a lack of it—was the cause of the sadness in this woman's face. She really was extraordinarily beautiful. Her eyes were so large and a crystalline blue. Like the sky over Mongolia, except with the shadow of…what?

He blinked, abruptly realizing he had lost control of his thoughts and was staring at her. What was he doing here? Oh, yes. Tracy. Tigress training. "She's with Nathan?" he murmured out loud. "But we were to be partners. Why would she choose him?"

The girl stared at him, and he realized that she had lost all the awe in her gaze. "I told you—they love each other."

He shook his head, unable to process the most basic of information. He had to repeat it out loud just to push it through his foggy brain. "Tracy chose Nathan. Not me."

The girl arched a brow at him. "Pretty full of yourself, aren't you?"

Stephen frowned, not understanding her slang. "With Tracy as my partner, we would have attained the heights of Tantric ecstasy together. Nathan is not a dragon master. He can't give her what I can."

She stared at him, her head tilted to one side. "Maybe he can give her something else. Like *love.*"

Stephen just shook his head. If Tracy had chosen the earthly path with Nathan then it would do no good to argue. Many tigresses made the mistake of falling in love. And yet, he was here. He could at least talk to her, maybe try to change her mind. "She did not seem stupid," he murmured.

"Wow, you are really not helping yourself here."

He frowned, his jet-lagged mind struggling to follow her strange words. "I have always done my ancestors great honor. I am named after my great-grandfather who was a pig farmer. Every day I light incense to honor his legacy."

She waved a hand at his rumpled designer suit and expensive Italian loafers. "Pig farmers must do really well in China."

He frowned. She didn't understand what he was saying. "My family no longer raises pigs. We package, ship and export pork. I meant only that I honor his legacy." As he spoke, his vision blurred gray. He blinked rapidly and within moments normal sight returned, but he was still startled by it. He was too young to be this tired.

Meanwhile, the blond woman released a roll of laughter that filled the air. It was light and musical, and it felt like a fresh breeze in the gloomy hallway. "I'm sure Great-granddad is filled with pride."

He stared at her, his mind struggling to keep up. There had been power in the girl's laugh. Yin power that had shivered through his spine and into his groin. Who was she? "I need to speak with Nathan. My cell phone doesn't work in the United States."

"So you're that big dragon teacher who was supposed to partner Tracy? But since she's with Nathan now, you must be free."

He nodded. Tracy and he had been matched on all levels—body, personality and expertise. Together, they would spend many days and nights in pursuit of a mystical experience. It would begin with physical stimulation, but it would lead to so much more. They had been just about to begin their practice. When she suddenly left the temple in Hong Kong to follow Nathan back here to the University of Illinois, Stephen had followed, of course. Tracy was too talented a tigress to release without a fight. "I am Stephen Chu, lead dragon at the Tigress Temple."

"Your great-grandfather's name was *Stephen?*" The girl's lips quirked at the edges, and he noticed for the first time how nicely formed her mouth was. He was so lost in admiration of the curve and color of her lips that he nearly missed her next words. "Your *Chinese* grandfather?"

She looked at him. He looked back. His English was excellent, but when he was this tired, he tended to lag a couple sentences behind. "What? No. His name was Xin Tian. Stephen is my English name."

"Okey-dokey. Welcome to the U.S., Mr. Stephen Chu. My name is Zoe Lewis, and I'm one of Nathan's students." She smiled at him. "And since Tracy is off the partner list, are you interested in anyone else?"

He swallowed, his mind rolling through the possibilities. Zoe obviously had intriguing potential, but nothing was ever simple in the pursuit of heaven. Neophytes always wanted to partner with him because he was the handsome rich guy. They weren't interested in advancing their spirit or attaining heaven. They just wanted inside his wallet. He might risk it with this woman, but then there was the other problem: temple politics. He couldn't just pick a girl because she was here. That wasn't the way things were done in the Tigress Temple.

"Are you all right?"

He blinked, stunned to realize he'd been staring at her

again. And given her expression, he hadn't looked as though he was lost in her beauty. "I need to talk to Nathan."

"He'll be here in a minute. I'm waiting for him, too, but my guess is he's out of the teaching business. I can't imagine an engaged man doing some of the things he talked about. At least not with anyone but Tracy."

She pushed to her feet, and even this tired he could see that her body qualified her as a partner. She had high breasts and well-formed legs beneath her faded jeans, though she seemed a bit too muscular to have a proper willow waist. With better clothing, she could compare very well to other tigresses. Better yet, she appeared much more adult now that she wasn't sitting cross-legged on the floor. He'd guess she was in her mid-twenties.

"So are you here to take on students?" she asked. "If so, we could figure out a lesson schedule now."

He shook his head. Clearly she didn't understand the temple structure. "I am a dragon master. I do not take students."

She frowned. "But you were going to take on Tracy, and she started after me."

"The Tigress Mother assigned us to be partners."

She tilted her head and her wispy blond hair fell like yellow silk across her shoulder. It was a simple gesture, obviously not meant as a seduction, and yet he found the sight mesmerizing.

"So how does one get assigned a partner?" she pressed.

"It is a complicated process," he said, irritated with himself for being tempted. He had precious little time. His business was falling down around his ears. The world economic crisis had hit the pork industry, too, which meant his corporation was on shaky ground. He'd slept less than two hours in two days, and his right-hand man, Shen Jiao Kai, was hoarse from screaming through the phone at him. Stephen might consider taking Zoe as a partner. She was certainly interesting enough, but it would require time and delicate handling to make the change. And first he had to be sure things were finished with Tracy. "Did you hear her say it? That she wishes to be married to Nathan?"

"No, I didn't." Zoe's voice was growing curt. He'd hurt her feelings, but he didn't have the brain power to smooth things over. "I got it from the lady in 2B," she continued. "So you're here to beg Tracy to pick you. Good luck with that." Her tone made it obvious that he didn't have a prayer.

He sighed, his gaze drawn back to her despite his intention. "She is deeply in love?" he asked. Love was the biggest pitfall for a tigress. And for most women, now that he thought about it. Why did normally sane women fall for such an obvious illusion?

Zoe was silent for a long time, her eyes flat and a little pitying as she scanned him from head to toe. He abruptly became aware of every wrinkle in his suit, every smudge on his shoes. "Yeah," she drawled. "But I'm sure she'd leave the love of a lifetime to run screaming for you." He couldn't miss the disdain in her tone.

"And you," he snapped back, "you are not a helpful person."

Her eyes widened in surprise. He could see he had scored a hit, and he was not quite sure why. He merely meant that she was not being helpful to him. It was not a character judgment, and yet she obviously took it as one. She squared her shoulders and glared venomously at him. "Well, sucks to be me then. I guess I'll just have to study in silence." She grabbed her textbook and slammed it open.

He frowned, trying to figure out how to make amends. He did not casually hurt other people. "I am sorry," he said. "It must be my English—"

"Your English is just fine, Mr. Chu. And *silence* means you have to be quiet, too."

He opened his mouth to respond, but shut it again at her glare. He was too exhausted to smooth over the situation now. Maybe it was for the best. He didn't have time to take on a partner now. He would go back to Hong Kong as soon as he verified Tracy's plans. So he folded his arms across his chest and leaned back against the wall with a huff. Ten minutes later, his eyes drifted shut.

ZOE LOOKED UP when the arrogant man started snoring. She'd never seen anyone sleep standing up before, but there he was—all wrinkled suit and sculpted beauty— snoring like he was crashed out on silk sheets.

Her heart softened a little toward him. He really did look wiped. As long as he didn't talk, she could pretend he wasn't an asshole. He certainly was nice to look at: rugged face, high cheekbones and straight black hair that was supposed to be slicked back. Right now it slipped forward across his forehead in stylish disarray. His shoulders were broad without being bulky, his hips lean, and in his dark suit—black pants, gray shirt, black tie—he looked like a movie-star bad boy.

Zoe sighed. Why did all the cute ones end up being jerks?

Her thoughts were cut off at the sounds of footsteps on the stairs. Pushing to her feet, she made it to the stairway railing and looked down. Three floors below, Nathan and Tracy were wrapped arm in arm, their heads tucked close together. Nathan chuckled softly, and Zoe felt her chest tighten in envy. They were probably talking about grocery shopping or something mundane, but their intimacy was almost painful to watch. She didn't know whether to pity them the disillusion to come or fervently pray for their happily ever after. Someone somewhere ought to get real love.

She had once believed in true love. She had gotten married and was happily looking forward to her picket fence and two or three kids. But her husband, Marty, turned out to be an idiot who lost all their money. Her dreams of happily ever after vaporized, and children… Her heart twisted painfully in her chest. Children just weren't in the cards for her. She'd ditched Marty the Moron, gone back to school, and very soon would graduate to begin a new life with her own dreams— completely free of stupid men.

There'd just been one glitch. Her housemate Janet had given her a gift of Tantric classes with Nathan Gao. Zoe hadn't expected anything earth-shattering, but there was something in the practice that appealed to her. It grounded her in her body and released all her sexual hang-ups on a level she couldn't begin to explain. And then, damn it, her teacher fell in love with Tracy and had stopped teaching.

Rather than dwell on her bad luck, Zoe gathered her things and met the lovers halfway down the stairs. Action was her new motto and, in this case, an easy bulwark against loneliness.

"Hey, lovebirds," she called, smiling when they hastily broke apart. "You got a visitor upstairs. Stephen Chu."

Both Nathan and Tracy gasped—and wasn't that just too cute?—but apparently for different reasons.

"Zoe!" Nathan cried. "I completely forgot our lesson."

"Stephen!" Tracy grimaced. "What's he doing here?"

"Not a problem," Zoe answered Nathan. "I got some homework done. And near as I can tell," she added to Tracy, "he's here to lure you away." Thankfully, there wasn't a trace of envy in her voice. But really, why did Tracy get two guys desperate to have her?

"Oh, crap," Tracy moaned. "I told him I wasn't interested."

Zoe shrugged. "He doesn't seem like a guy who understands the word *no*. Probably doesn't hear it that often."

Meanwhile, Nathan was switching into teacher mode. "Did you read the book I gave you? I'm afraid it'll be hard for me to partner with you for the more advanced—"

"Don't worry," Zoe interrupted. "I read. I learned. And I understand that engaged men really shouldn't be 'polishing the mirror' with someone other than their fiancées."

A male voice cut through from above. "Polishing the mirror is done between two female partners."

Everyone looked up to see Stephen standing like a god at the top of the stairs. From this angle, he looked tall and imposing, but Zoe remembered the wrinkles in his suit and the very human weariness on his features. "Thank you, Mr. Webster, I'll make sure to use the phrase correctly in the future." She didn't know whether to laugh or cry when he just looked at her with that blank uncomprehending stare.

Meanwhile, Nathan mounted the stairs with surprising speed. "Is something wrong at the temple? Is my mother—"

"She's fine. Everyone is fine," Stephen answered as he rubbed a hand over his face, further rumpling his hair. "Nothing wrong." Then he blinked and slowly turned his focus to Tracy. He made a visible effort to pull himself together, straightening his shoulders, softening his gaze and shifting his tones to more cultured accents. "Hello, Tracy. You left Hong Kong too quickly for me to talk to you."

Seduction mode, and wow, was it potent. Liquid brown eyes, bedroom voice and enough handsome features to grace a movie marquee. No wonder the guy was arrogant. He probably had women wetting themselves just for a minute of his attention. Zoe wasn't immune, and she'd already decided the guy was a jerk. Even Tracy, who was desperately in love with Nathan, blushed and looked away.

"I'm sorry," she murmured. "I told you I couldn't do it."

Stephen sighed. "So you have chosen love." He sounded like she'd chosen baloney over pâté.

Tracy raised her eyes to meet his with clear purpose. "Yes, and don't knock it," she said, her gaze sliding to Nathan. "You'd be surprised what partners in love can accomplish."

Stephen remained silent, clearly mulling over her words. In the end, he just rubbed a hand over his face in defeat. "Very well. Felicitations to you both." Then he turned and grabbed his garment bag before heading down the stairs.

"Wait!" Nathan called. "Zoe is ready for her first partner. I don't know how long you're staying, but if you could manage a few sessions with her, I'd be grateful."

Stephen paused to look down at Zoe, and she damned herself for holding her breath in hope. Sure, he was an arrogant jerk, but he was also damned sexy. Who wouldn't want a fling with a Chinese aristocrat? He was dark and exotic, and she thought she caught a spark of interest in his eyes.

But then he turned away, looking back over his shoulder at Nathan. "I'm leaving on the next plane."

Zoe's chest tightened against his cold words, but she still managed to give voice to her anger. "You're an ass. I don't want you as a partner."

He turned back to her, his gaze catching hers and holding. She lifted her chin, putting every ounce of bravado she possessed into staring him down. Let him see what he was missing! She waited. One heartbeat. Two. Three.

He shrugged and brushed past her. It was the ultimate dismissal, and Zoe felt her soul shrivel into nothing. Stephen was just one more in a long line of men who couldn't be bothered with her. Was something wrong with her that she could only attract idiots like her ex? She lifted her hand to her chest—to that spot right above her heart—and rubbed at the pain blossoming there.

"Oh, God, Zoe—I'm sorry," Tracy babbled. "He didn't mean that like it sounded."

Nathan agreed. "He can be really cold sometimes. His crappy parents never taught him anything about being kind."

"Save it," Zoe said. "I don't care." She gathered what dignity she could and turned to Nathan. "I don't think this stuff is for me right now. Thanks anyway." She started down the steps.

"Zoe, wait—" Nathan called.

Zoe couldn't stop. If she did, she'd shatter, and she didn't have the strength to glue herself back together again. But Tracy wasn't to be deterred. She ran down the stairs, catching up with Zoe on the second-floor landing.

"Don't give up," she said. "We'll get you a teacher."

Zoe paused, wanting to brush off all this Tantric

energy stuff as unimportant. But her initial classes had taught her something. She had *felt* something, and that hadn't happened in so very long. She really did want to keep learning, but not at the expense of everything else. And then there was the other big problem. "Truthfully, I can't afford it. My lessons were a gift from my house-mate. I just don't have the money to keep going."

"We'll work something out," Tracy insisted. "This stuff is worth pursuing. Believe me, no one is more sur-prised than me, but Zoe…" She swallowed, and mo-mentarily lifted her gaze up to Nathan. Love filled her expression, making her entire body seem to glow. "It's worth it, I swear. Just give us some time to find you the right partner."

Zoe was startled by the flash of yearning in her heart. At one time, she had thought Nathan was the perfect partner for her. But then Tracy had burst into their class, and that was it for anyone else. And now? She sighed, trying to dredge up some hope for herself. Did she really think she could find something meaningful with a man? Her heart said yes, but her mind said no. No man. No children. These were the facts of her life.

"It's just not meant for me," she said softly, then turned away.

2

STEPHEN SIPPED HIS espresso, fully engaging all of his senses. He appreciated the brew's dark color, smelled the rich scent and then allowed the bitter taste to expand across his tongue and through his mouth. He rolled the heat to the back of his throat, then took his time swallowing. Then he breathed—deeply, consciously and with renewed caffeine in his body. A smile curved his lips as a sense of calm expanded from his groin outward, bringing serenity to every part of his body. This was his morning ritual, and he relished it. Of course, it was the middle of the afternoon in Champaign, Illinois, but that didn't negate the experience.

Unfortunately, his caffeine glow was short-lived as worries intruded. He should be on his way back to Hong Kong. He ought to be on the phone right now with his executive vice president Shen Jiao Kai figuring out how to stop the latest hemorrhage in the company's finances. But after collapsing in the nearest hotel last night, he'd woken in the grips of a wet dream the likes of which he hadn't experienced since…since ever. Not even as a teen. He didn't remember what had set his heart to pounding and his organ to rock-hard thrusting, except that it centered on the blond woman Zoe. He had dismissed the notion at first. The dream was probably the result of too little sleep and too many time zones. But he couldn't get her out of his mind. And he couldn't get back to sleep. Not until he had contacted Nathan and found out how he could get in touch with the woman.

So now he sat in this vintage café on campus waiting for her to walk by after her class. It made no sense. It was just a dream, after all. But even so, he had showered and dressed with meticulous care, then rushed out, stopping long enough to buy a dozen roses before making his way to this dingy booth in a secluded corner. He didn't even know what he wanted to say to the woman, but he knew he had to see her again.

His wish was granted before he'd finished his second demitasse. She was tucked in the middle of a group of students rushing along the concrete pathways. Her blond hair was pressed flat beneath a cap, and she looked cold as she hunched into her thin jacket. He was on his feet in a moment. Something about her tiny frame drew him as nothing else.

He rushed out, gritting his teeth against the cold November wind. There wasn't even snow on the ground, but the chill went straight through him, especially his hands. "Zoe!" he called. "Zoe!"

Her expression turned into a tight frown as she spied him.

"Please wait!" he said as he made it to her side. "Please, these are for you. So I can apologize."

She glanced in puzzlement at the flowers. "They're going to die. It's too cold for roses out here."

He was confused. This was not the way that women usually responded to a gift of roses. Obviously, he had quite a steep road to climb with her. So he smoothed out his expression and tried to look contrite. "Then let us go inside where they will be warm." He gestured to the café behind them. "Allow me to buy you a cup of coffee. We can talk in private there."

She raised her eyebrows. "Isn't that café a little... um...low-end for you? You don't think your Italian shoes will be damaged just from contact with the floor?"

Did everyone believe he reviled anything but the very best? He certainly liked Italian leather. Who didn't? But he'd spent weeks in places that made central Illinois look like paradise. Did anyone realize that pork farms in China were rarely beautiful? That he had rolled up his sleeves and worked on farm after farm when he was younger? It had been one of his father's requirements before he turned over the business.

"I wish to go wherever you will feel most comfortable," he said honestly. "A café, a pigpen, an expensive restaurant—I don't care. What would make you happiest?"

"You think I would be happy in a pigpen?" she snapped. "Is that supposed to impress me?"

He blinked, confused by her attitude. "I did not mean to insult you," he said carefully. "Please tell me what to say to apologize."

She looked at him, her blue eyes large and troubled. Behind her, the traffic light changed and the crowd of students flowed past. He counted it a measure of success that she didn't cross with them. In the end, she sighed and her shoulders sagged. "Okay, now I'm the one being rude." She swallowed, her eyes going to the café behind him. "I'd die for a mocha and a sticky bun."

He lifted the half-frozen roses. "Death accomplished. Let me get you your reward."

ZOE FELT HER LIPS twitch in surprise at Stephen Chu's joke. She hadn't really thought he possessed a sense of humor, but obviously there was more to him than just a handsome exterior. After all, he'd bought her roses to apologize. The least she could do was let him buy her a cup of coffee.

As he escorted her into Café Paradiso, she wondered for a second time why a man who dressed in Italian loafers would deign to walk into a place like this. It just wasn't posh enough for him.

Clearly she was wrong, she thought as he bought her a large mocha and a sticky bun, adding an espresso for himself. It didn't even bother her that he ordered for her. She found it unexpectedly sweet. No one had ever acted the gentleman around her. At best, the men in her life treated her with casual disregard. At worst... Well, Marty was her ex now, so she wasn't going to think about him. Especially when she had a handsome man trying to apologize to her.

She settled into the booth, almost wincing at the thought of those fine white linen shirtsleeves on the linoleum tabletop. She didn't see any grease smears, but who knew what had been spilt on these tables?

She wanted to break the ice somehow, but what should she say? What could the two of them possibly have in common? She chose silence and took a careful sip of her mocha.

Chocolate slid over her tongue and heat expanded through her mouth and throat. She hadn't eaten at all today and this was a triple assault of chocolate, heat and caffeine. She stifled a purr of delight, but her body betrayed her. She shuddered in pleasure but then her stomach started to cramp. That often happened when she hadn't eaten in a while, and she had to wait out the pain with short panting breaths.

It took forever. She kept her eyes downcast. Even tore off a piece of her pastry, then chewed it extra slowly to cover her discomfort. But when she finally looked up, she saw his eyes dark and troubled on her. He didn't say a word, but stood up and quickly crossed to the counter where a pitcher of water and glasses sat. He poured a large glass and brought it back, placing it before her.

She took it gratefully, drinking down a few swallows. Finally her stomach eased. "Thank you," she whispered when she could speak.

"There are people in China with whom I work. I always take them out to dinner when I visit because I know how poor they are. I have to remind them over and over to eat slowly and drink a lot of tea. An empty stomach requires care."

She blinked and pulled out her most ditzy-blond expression. "I knew I forgot to do something—eat!" she trilled.

His expression didn't crack. Instead, he dipped his chin in acknowledgment and took a sip of his drink. Did he buy her stupid-blond routine? She doubted it. But apparently he was kind enough to let her pretend. Ashamed of her own poverty—especially when compared to this man's obvious wealth—she tore another piece off the bun.

"I suppose you are wondering why I went to such pains to find you," he said. His voice was low and intimate, and she couldn't resist looking back up at him just to watch his lips move. He was that beautiful. "I was an ass yesterday. I hadn't slept, and I was unbearably rude. I hope you can forgive me."

She smiled. She couldn't help it; he seemed so contrite.

"Apology accepted. But a simple 'I'm sorry' would have sufficed. You didn't have to buy me anything."

"Perhaps, but I wanted to beg a favor of you as well. And I always find that chocolate and roses are the best way to soften up a woman."

She raised her eyebrows. "Really? The *best* way to soften a woman?"

His cheeks lifted in a slow smile. "No, not the *best* way, but perhaps the first step—a prelude to something better."

She felt her face heat. Was she actually flirting with this man? This rude, arrogant, Chinese aristocrat of a man? Apparently so, because she took another drink of her mocha while flashing him a look over the rim of the cup. Then again, why not flirt with an unattainable man? It was the safest form of play.

"In that case," she added with a wink, "feel free to insult me anytime."

"In order to do that, I would need you to say yes to my request."

She leaned back in her seat, suspicion souring her thoughts. He probably needed her to do his laundry or something. "Mr. Chu, I don't know that—"

"Stephen. Please call me Stephen."

She shook her head, unaccountably tired. Yesterday, she might have played with him. Yesterday, she might have listened to whatever he proposed and entered into it with a sense of fun. But after she'd left him, she'd returned home to find that she'd been robbed. She'd gone from a tight budget to dead broke within the space of a few hours. She knew exactly who had taken her money: Marty. She'd even filed a police report, but that didn't make any difference. As of today, she couldn't afford to play with Mr. Chu, no matter how handsome he was. So she finished the last of her sticky bun and lifted her mocha, startled to find the cup empty.

"Thank you so much for the food, Mr. Chu." She glanced over his shoulder at the clock. "But I've got a ton of homework to do." And she hoped to could catch a couple of hours of sleep before reporting to work at the Bread Café at 4:00 a.m.

He straightened in alarm. "But you haven't heard my request."

"Have a nice flight back to Hong Kong," she said by way of answer. "I'm sorry we couldn't spend more time together," she added, startled because she meant it.

He reached out, grabbing her arm. The gesture wasn't rough or even painful. A simple touch to stop her from leaving, but she reacted instinctively, throwing his arm wide and slamming her other arm forward to catch him under the chin. She stopped just before snapping his windpipe, not because she held back, but because he countered her move with a swiftness that left her reeling. He'd simultaneously pulled back and knocked her arm aside so that she punched the air above his shoulder.

Then she realized what she'd done. If he'd been one smidgen slower, she could have killed him. "Oh, my God! Oh, my God!" she gasped. "I'm so sorry! I'm sorry, sorry, sorry! Oh, God!" She shifted her stricken gaze to the other people in the café. They were all watching her with various degrees of interest. "My bad. I'm fine. Honest."

He straightened slowly, coming to stand in front of her with his brows furrowed in anger. "No apology necessary," he said slowly. "I should not have startled you like that. A woman alone in this world needs to feel protected. I commend you on your fighting skill."

She flushed, stupidly warmed by the compliment,

even though she was still mortified by her actions. "I'm sorry," she babbled. "I've never done that before. It was all my fault. And after last night, I'm so jumpy—" She abruptly shut her mouth. The last thing she needed to do was start spilling her life story. Though it was nice to know that her self-defense classes had taken. "I'm so sorry, Mr. Chu. Please forgive me."

He was buttoning his jacket, his expression unreadable. "I think perhaps that I do not forgive you, Zoe," he said softly. "I think perhaps that I will demand an apology from you."

She frowned, hunching her shoulders as she pulled on her backpack. "I am sorry. Really—"

"Over dinner. I demand you apologize to me over dinner."

She realized what he was doing. He was simply trying to get her to go to dinner with him, but she shook her head. "You are a lot nicer than I thought," she admitted.

He raised his finely sculpted eyebrows, but didn't comment.

"And I really am sorry. But I can't—"

"Zoe, I need to talk to you." He kept his voice low, and his eyes seemed so sincere. "Allow me to take you to dinner. I am in a bit of a quandary, and I really need your help."

She stared at him. Who used words like *quandary?* "I'm sure I can't help you with whatever problem you have. I'm…" Why did he make her say it? "I just don't think I'm in your league."

He blinked, clearly not understanding the reference. Then he rubbed his hand over his face in a gesture of pure masculine exhaustion. "I am not doing this well."

Join the club, she thought with a wry smile. "It's something in the Illinois air. Screws us all up at some point."

He blinked at her, then apparently got the joke because his lips softened into a smile. "I can help you," he said. "Whatever has been so difficult, I think I can help you."

She was sure he could. He obviously had money to spare, and she could use some of it. But no one gave money away for free, and she couldn't afford the strings. "I've got everything under control," she lied. "Thank you again for the coffee. And the roses." Then she turned and headed for the door. He followed.

"Give me your phone number. I must have a way to contact you."

She looked up at him, and for a moment allowed herself to indulge in the fantasy. Wouldn't it be great to have an international magnate boyfriend? Wouldn't it be amazing just once to allow herself to be wined and dined by a god of a man?

But then reality hit with another painful stomach cramp. Even if he was willing, when would she fit him into her schedule? Now that she was broke, she had to up her hours at the Bread Café. She had a heavy load of classes to finish her MBA degree, which meant homework up the wazoo. Even if she believed a Chinese aristocrat could be interested in her—which she absolutely did not—how could she find the time?

She couldn't. "I don't have a phone, Mr. Chu. I can't afford one." And with that she walked out of the café. Too bad she couldn't walk out on her thoughts while she was at it. Despite her best efforts, the fantasy lingered in her mind.

Thankfully, her accounting homework would be enough to squelch all lingering dreams. With a sigh, she hunched against the cold and headed home.

3

ACCOUNTING DID NOT hold her attention. Nathan had often spoken about manifesting her desires. Whatever she thought about—be it good or bad—would materialize if she put enough of her female yin energy behind the thoughts. Therefore, it was no surprise when Stephen Chu appeared at the door of her boardinghouse. After all, she'd been fantasizing about him for hours now, so of course he would be standing there holding out bags of takeout from at least three different restaurants.

One of her housemates—Janet—had opened the door to him while Zoe watched from a couch near the fireplace in the front lounge. Stephen hadn't even blinked at Janet's perky breasts, barely hidden beneath a thin tank. He passed over her friend's seductive makeup and lush Italian physique to scan the room for Zoe. When he saw her on the couch, his smile was warm and so intimate that her heart stopped beating for a moment. Then he hefted his bags and spoke with smooth elegance.

"Hello. I bring food for Miss Zoe Lewis."

She wanted to leap up from the couch and kiss him senseless.

Meanwhile Janet glanced nervously in Zoe's direction. "Um, I'll have to see if she's here."

Stephen frowned. "But she is sitting right there."

Janet dropped her hands on her hips in a militant gesture. "Yeah, buster, but that doesn't mean she wants to speak with you. We protect our own here."

Stephen raised an eyebrow at her sudden aggression, but didn't comment. Instead he looked to Zoe. "Are you at home, Zoe?"

She thought about saying no. She had already invested too much time—and fantasy energy—in this man. But at that moment, the scents of his food offerings wafted over to her. Her stomach rumbled. As did Janet's.

Zoe smiled. "I guess I am. Janet, you hungry? It looks like Stephen brought enough for the whole house!"

Her friend grinned. "I'm starved!" Then she stepped back far enough for Stephen to enter, neatly relieving him of his bags as she did. But then she paused, her body tensing warily. "So he's, like, on the approved list, right? He's not somebody sent by your ex to steal your rent money again, right?"

Zoe winced. Sometimes her housemate had way too big a mouth. "Yes, I think we're safe for the moment."

Just as she feared, Stephen arched a very sexy eyebrow and asked the obvious question. "Was there a theft?"

"Oh, yeah!" Janet gabbed as she started pulling out boxes of food. "I let in her ex yesterday, and I am so, so sorry—"

"It's okay, Janet—" Zoe interrupted.

"I mean, she told us before, but I just forgot. But I swear I'll never forget now—"

"It's over, Janet—" Zoe tried again.

"And he took all her money!"

Zoe sighed. "It wasn't *all* my money." Just her rent money. She turned to Stephen. "My parents gave me a Visa gift card for my birthday. I'd planned to use it for my rent."

"Your…ex stole it?"

She shrugged. "He doesn't really think of it as stealing."

Janet huffed as she continued setting out food. "He came in and stole your birthday present. But there's no proof, you know. The cops have talked to him and all, but the card's gone and it's all my fault because I let the jerk in here, and oooo! Lasagna! Is there garlic bread?"

Stephen flowed easily with the shift in conversation, but his eyes looked anxious as he watched Zoe. "The bread is over there. I didn't know what you'd like, so I got a little of everything."

"Wow! Chinese, too!" Janet squealed. Then she picked up a clear plastic container. "Oh, here's a cheeseburger. Zoe loves cheeseburgers."

No, actually, Zoe loved lasagna, but Janet was already scooping it up with typical zest. Janet's emotions had no boundaries. She could be unexpectedly generous, like when she impulsively bought Zoe a dozen Tantric classes with Nathan. Or incredibly self-centered. Most people ended up drawing clear lines where the girl was concerned, but Zoe didn't have the heart to do it. Janet was the ditzy younger sister she'd never had. Besides, hanging out with her made Zoe feel young. So she smiled and took the cheeseburger. Or she did until Stephen put his hand out.

"Is that what you really want, Zoe? There is a great deal of food here. I would like you to choose whatever pleases you most." His eyes were dark and serious, his manner completely chivalrous. And most of all, his attention was focused completely and totally on her. It wasn't just his eyes. Everything—his stance, his voice, even his breath—seemed to be centered on her.

It was shocking and completely overpowering. There wasn't anything sexual in his attitude, but that total awareness was completely new. Who looked at a person like that? As if no one else in the world mattered? What would it be like to make love with this man? To be the center of his attention through the most intimate of acts? She looked at his mouth and barely restrained herself from leaping off the couch and attacking him.

Janet, on the other hand, wasn't nearly so restrained. "Oooo, wow. That is so awesomely sweet. Why can't I meet guys like you?"

And still Stephen didn't move. His eyes were on Zoe as she felt her face heating to incandescent. "Um," she finally managed. "The burger is great."

He waited a moment, as if judging her words. Could he see that she was lying? But he didn't question her. Instead, he nodded and passed her the plastic box. She felt herself flush even darker. How amazing was it that he allowed her to choose? It wasn't his fault that Janet had snatched up the lasagna. He'd let her choose, and better yet, hadn't challenged her response. In short, he treated her as an adult, and that moved him into a very select category in her life.

Even her parents still thought of her as a little girl who needed to be protected, not a grown woman who could make it on her own. Then came Marty, who always assumed he knew better than she did. And since she'd been intent on her picket fence and children, she had allowed him to take charge. It was only when the creditors started calling that Zoe realized Marty was not the financial genius he pretended to be. Of course, by that time she was in such deep debt that her parents had to help pay her rent.

But that was then. This was now, and so she smiled

at her exotic Chinese god. "Please, sit down," she said, her eyes—and her thoughts—on his too-sexy mouth.

He turned to look at the easy chair to her right, but Janet plopped herself in it with a surreptitious wink. Clearly, she was matchmaking, since the only other space was on the couch with Zoe. Stephen flashed a smile then settled in the middle of the couch, close enough to touch her, but not quite doing it. Not yet. But she knew he was thinking about it. She certainly was.

"What would you like to eat?" she asked.

He looked over the selection. "I believe I will try your American version of Chinese food."

Janet snorted. "Don't expect much. Not if you're used to the real thing." She took a big bite of lasagna. "So are you a visiting professor here or something?"

He shook his head. "I came all the way from Hong Kong to find Zoe," he said.

"Ooo!" Janet cooed, her eyes huge.

Zoe did everything but choke on her food. If that wasn't a whopper of a lie, she didn't know what was.

"I can see you don't believe me," he said softly. "But it's true."

"You came for Tracy."

"I came for a partner. I thought it was Tracy, but I was wrong."

Zoe took her time swallowing a bite of her food. It was a really good burger, but she barely noticed it. Instead, she watched him. But for the life of her, she couldn't read his expression. "I thought you didn't take students," she said coolly.

"I don't. I take partners." Then he cocked an eyebrow. "Or I do for a little bit. Eventually I will have to go back home."

Janet leaned forward. "Partner in what? Student for what?"

No way was Zoe going to answer that one. But apparently, Stephen had an answer for everything.

"Asian religion. I am a student of a particular form—"

"A master, you mean," Zoe drawled.

"And I need a partner to complete some of the forms. I was hoping that you would help me," he said to her. "I would be extraordinarily grateful."

"Wow," breathed Janet. "What kind of religion?"

Zoe felt her face heating, but couldn't see a way out of this. Janet wasn't one to let things pass. If she found out that Stephen was talking about a sexual ritual, there would be no end to the teasing.

Then, smooth as could be, Stephen smiled. "It is a form of tai chi. The body moves energy through certain forms."

Janet wrinkled her nose. "You mean that stuff old people do in China? Like morning exercise?"

Stephen didn't answer. He simply shrugged, but his lips said something else. Were they curved in…mischief? He flashed Zoe a look that was definitely part devil, and she felt her heart flutter in excitement.

Fortunately, Janet didn't see it. "Too bad it's boring stuff. Wouldn't it be more fun if it were sex rites or something?" Then before anyone could respond, her cell phone chimed in with a bad version of "Fur Elise." "Oh! That's for me!" she cried as she leaped up from the easy chair. "Thanks for the lasagna. It was great!"

A moment later, Zoe and Stephen were alone. The lounge where they were sitting was right off the front hallway. People would be going in and out on a regular basis. If she listened hard, she could still hear Janet chatting on her cell phone about physics homework.

And yet, here in this corner, she felt completely secluded—intimate, even—with Stephen. And that made her surprisingly excited. Good Lord, even the skin nearest him seemed to tingle with awareness. How bizarre was that? And she couldn't stop looking at his mouth. She wanted to kiss him that badly!

"Happy birthday," he said softly.

She blinked, then flushed, abruptly looking away. She ended up staring at his hands. One was holding a container of beef and snow peas, his fingers long and elegant around the white box. The other held chopsticks with the same easy grace with which he did everything.

"Uh-um," she stammered. "Thank you."

"Did you have a party?"

She nearly laughed. "Not at my age. You don't celebrate so much when you're about a decade older than everyone else. Don't get me wrong. I adore them, but they'd faint if they knew how old I really am."

He raised his eyebrows. "They do seem very young. Why do you live with them?"

She stared at him, stunned by the question. Could he really not guess? "Because it's all I can afford."

He shook his head. "There are plenty of cheap places to live that would allow more privacy. You chose a house full of people. Why?"

She bit her lip, stunned by his perception. He was right. There were other places she could live just as cheaply. "I like them. They may be young, but they're nice."

"And you thought there was more safety in numbers, perhaps?" He leaned forward. "Did you learn self-defense because of your ex? Did he hurt you?"

Her eyes widened in shock. This man noticed things well beyond...well, anyone she'd ever met.

"Marty never hurt me," she said softly. "He just thinks we're still married. That he can come and take my stuff because it's *our* stuff. But it isn't, no matter what he thinks."

"How long have you been divorced?"

"We separated two years ago. I dumped him and started graduate school in the very same year." She sighed. "The divorce took a while, but it's done now."

"So you chose to live with these girls as a way to be safe?"

She shrugged. "Maybe. But I was lonely, too."

"Surely you have a lot of friends?"

She shook her head. "Between working and school, there hasn't been time. My parents still think Marty's a prince, which he's not. And they really hate having a daughter who's divorced. A woman isn't whole without a husband, according to them. So…these girls became my family. They're my younger sisters." And maybe they were a little like the children she would never have. Not because she couldn't. All of her parts worked, as far as she knew, but it just wasn't in the plan. She was going to have a career with stability and wealth, and a future that no man could take away. There simply wasn't time to do all that *and* find a man *and* have children. "Anyway, I never did the whole college scene before. I wanted to try it."

"Do you like it?"

She looked into his dark eyes. She saw nothing there but honest inquiry. And she felt his attention so keenly, as if it slipped under her skin and set her whole body to simmer. He acted as if he had nothing else in the world to do but talk to her. But of course that wasn't true. It couldn't be true. He was an international mogul or something. And yet she couldn't stop herself from easing back into the couch, tucking her feet under her, and talking to him as if they were the closest of friends. Or lovers.

"Sometimes I think they're all so very young." She gestured at Janet in the hallway. She was jumping as she squealed into her phone. The sight made Zoe smile. "I'm glad I did it. In just a few months, I'll graduate, get a real job and say goodbye to this forever."

She looked at Stephen as he leaned back and extended his feet onto the coffee table. It was an odd sight to be sure. Italian loafers on a cheap, scarred coffee table. But he made it look like the most natural thing in the world. "What's your degree in?"

"Masters in the science of finance. It's a fancy MBA—"

"But with an emphasis on the more technical, science-minded and practical aspects. Impressive."

She smiled, pleased with the compliment. "I'm not done yet. Just another few months." She wondered what his feet looked like. Were they as sexy as the rest of him?

"So why study Tantrism?" he asked. "What brought you to Nathan?"

"It was a gift from Janet. So I started, and I liked it." She tilted her head, beginning to wonder about the questions. It was so easy to talk to him that she'd volunteered a lot more than she usually did. But now she noticed that she knew almost nothing about him. "I might ask the same thing of you. Why does a big-time businessman hang around doing breast circles?"

He snorted, obviously startled by the image. "I am a man. My practices focus on—"

"Yeah, I know where your practices focus." And the thought of him stroking his penis made her unexpectedly hot. Panting, flushed hot! "I was just teasing you," she managed to squeak out.

He sobered, his gaze dark and serious. "I like it when you tease," he finally said. "I like you more and more." She felt his hand touch her chin, lifting her face up to meet his gaze. She hadn't even seen his arm move, but there he was, stroking her cheek with his thumb, and she was hard-pressed to even breathe. "You seem so small, as if a breeze could knock you over. But I think you have already had a hard life, and you are still here. Strong and vital. I think people underestimate you."

Her eyes widened, shocked anew by his perception. But that was nothing compared to her physical reaction. Her body shivered at his touch, and the need to kiss him burned on her lips. But she held herself still. He had been such a jerk at first, but he'd bought her roses and now dinner. Did she dare trust her judgment with this man? Meanwhile, he trailed his thumb from her cheek to her mouth, stroking back and forth over her swelling lips.

"Do not be afraid," he said. "You are strong enough to handle everything. Of this, I am absolutely sure."

She gasped, her belly quivering with shock. If he had said that he would protect her or that God would provide, she would have laughed in his face. But he had spoken of her strength, giving her a validation she hadn't even known was missing. He thought she was strong! Strong enough to handle her messed-up, impoverished life! And the shock of that had her eyes watering with unshed tears.

He gasped and muttered something that sounded like a muffled Chinese curse. He thought he had said something wrong.

"No, no!" she gasped. "It's not you—"

"I have hurt you. I—"

"No—"

"But your eyes. You are—"

She kissed him. She had been wanting to forever, and it just seemed like the thing to do. And oh, God, it was good.

Of course, a Tantric master would kiss well. His lips had just the right amount of firmness, mixed with just enough softness. He allowed her to lead, not pushing for anything more than she wanted to give. She had flattened her mouth against his, a kind of headlong rush that mashed their lips together like awkward adolescents.

He shifted his hands to her shoulders, then down to her upper forearms, supporting her weight as he adjusted the way their lips touched. He didn't open his mouth more than a teasing fraction of an inch, but instead allowed her to move across his mouth of her own accord. She held there, feeling her lips against his, the intermingling of breath and the texture of his mouth. She was not an awkward teenager to grasp and grope at a man. She had control and, if nothing else, had read a stack of Tantric texts on the art of the kiss.

But reading about something was night and day from actually doing it. And she hadn't started this with anything like clear thought. He must think she was an idiot.

"Don't think, Zoe," he whispered against her lips. "Just do what comes naturally." Then he smiled, touching his tongue to her lips. "Let your mouth be your guide."

She smiled. How could she help it? She had practically attacked this man, and now he was teasing her? She wanted to say something clever. She wanted to show him she was sophisticated and classy and completely exciting. But the truth was, he was the amazing one. He knew how to wait for her, to move at just the right moment to encourage her, but otherwise to let her lead.

She touched her lips to his, and he lifted himself toward her, allowing her full access. She stroked backward and forward across his mouth, and he held his breath in seeming awe, as if he wanted to hold on to every moment of their kiss. She extended her tongue to lick every millimeter of his mouth, and he smiled, clearly enjoying her exploration.

Then she pushed her tongue forward into his mouth. She had never done that before. Always, the man had thrust into her. She always received. But this time, she was the one touching his teeth, his tongue. What a difference it was! To be the one to thrust, pushing in and pulling out, while he received. He toyed, and he played with her as long as she wanted, then allowed her to withdraw.

It was amazing! Before long, she was wet with excitement. Her breath was coming in short pants, and…and she was practically lying on top of him on the couch. His hands had slid to her hips, and she was cradled against his groin. Good Lord, was that his erection? He was huge! And yet, she couldn't stop herself from breathing deeply, consciously pushing her abdominal muscles against him. He shuddered in response.

She had made him shudder!

"Please," he rasped against her cheek. "Please say we can partner. For a little bit. As long as you like. We can teach each other so much."

She had never heard such a heartfelt plea in her life. And, oh, she wanted to do it. "How?" she asked. Then she ignored his answer as she lowered her head to touch her lips to his neck. The skin was rougher here with his beard, and she needed to feel the texture against her tongue.

"We open energy channels first," he rasped. She nipped lightly at his neck and was pleased to feel him gasp.

"And then?" she asked as she opened her mouth wider to trail her teeth along the hard ridge of his jaw.

"Then?" He swallowed. Was she interfering with his ability to think? It certainly seemed so, and the idea made her more daring. She rolled her body higher up on his chest, making sure her pelvis dragged against his erection. He shuddered again, and she grinned. Then she leaned down to whisper into his ear.

"After we open energy channels, what happens then?"

"We get the energy to flow. Um, to move. To…ah…to…"

"To orgasm?"

"To pump! That is the word. The energy pumps higher and higher."

She raised her eyebrows at his clear confusion. She had read the texts. She knew exactly what they were supposed to do. They would stimulate each other as a way to raise their souls' vibrations. If they vibrated high enough, they would experience something heavenly.

She hadn't believed it at first. Truly, she had thought this was a whole bunch of hype built around really good sex. But during the beginning exercises, she had felt something, so she was willing to explore further. She was open to wandering in the sexual wilds for a while with this man. Why not? Her last great fling before she got a real job and a real life. A Tantric orgasm was supposed to be the height of physical ecstasy.

"You are certified as healthy, right?" she asked. "No diseases or anything?"

He clearly made an effort to focus. "Absolutely. I have brought papers from my doctor if you wish to—"

"I believe you," she said as she placed her mouth against his. She didn't want to hear about the doctor's reports he'd brought to prove his health to Tracy. She wanted to believe in this moment and the illusion of their intimacy.

"And you?" he asked when she eased off her attentions to his mouth. "Healthy?"

"Very."

His hands gripped her hips with a sudden fierceness. "Then we are agreed? We will partner?"

"Yes," she said.

He grinned and ground his groin against hers in a circular motion. This time, she was the one who shuddered. "Do we go to your room? Or will you come to my suite?" He glanced significantly toward the hallway. "We will have more privacy at my hotel."

She looked over to see that Janet and two more of her housemates were watching and giggling. Zoe felt her cheeks burn fever-hot. She'd completely forgotten where she was and who could see.

"Your suite," she gasped. "Definitely your suite."

He smiled, his eyes darkening as his hands gripped her hips, but he didn't say anything and he didn't move. She stilled, looking into his eyes, wondering what was wrong. Then she saw it. It was in his eyes, in the hard granite of his jaw, and the chiseled perfection of his face. Up until this moment, she had seen him as urbane: handsome, rich, but ultimately a little soft.

Not now. Now she saw the dragon master in him. She felt his power vibrate in the air between them. It was energy, charged enough to make every cell in her body tingle. And, oh, what it did to her breasts and groin. She was on fire.

"Is it always like this?" she gasped.

"Sweet Zoe, it has only begun."

4

STEPHEN CUPPED ZOE'S elbow as he escorted her into the cab. And what a backward city this was that he had to call for a cab rather than just hail one passing on the street. But that was unimportant now. In truth, it had given him time to think while he waited and Zoe packed a small bag.

He was still trembling! Sweet heaven, how could that be? Even with the goddess-on-earth Tracy, he had not held on to his excitement so long. Tracy had aroused him. Zoe infused him! Tracy was stimulating, but ten minutes out of her presence and he was able to lose himself in his work. The idea of ten minutes away from Zoe gripped his chest in a vice of fear.

How could this be? Two Tantric goddesses in Illinois? The odds were astronomical. The Tigress Mother scoured the globe looking for tigresses to train. And yet, he had never reacted to a woman as he did to Zoe. Never.

He looked sideways now at the petite blonde on the cab seat. She was gripping a heavy backpack of books and a tiny satchel of clothes. Her eyes were huge, her face pale, and if he wasn't mistaken, she was clenching the rope ties of the bag like a lifeline. She was clearly nervous, but her pointed nipples told him she was still aroused. He was, too, damn it.

What the hell did she have that she affected him so? She was a waif of a girl! But there was steel beneath her, a determination he hadn't expected. And a vulnerability that touched him. But why, why, why? He'd known beautiful women before, even blond ones. He'd known women with more underlying strength than Zoe and ones with more vulnerability.

Perhaps that was the key. All the women he knew were either vulnerable or strong, not both. No one managed the balance that he saw in Zoe. And sweet heaven, the package made him harder than granite.

He had to know if it were true, if she were indeed a goddess the likes of which the world had rarely seen. It would only take one night for him to know. And if she was, then nothing on Earth would keep him away from her.

ZOE TRIED NOT TO react as Stephen lifted her heavy backpack off her shoulders. He raised his eyebrows in surprise at the weight of her books, but she merely shrugged. Did he think that textbooks were light?

The exterior hotel doors whooshed opened, and Zoe damned herself for jumping. She'd been walking through automatic doors all her life, and here she was shying like a skittish rabbit. She was living a fantasy here. How many women got to have Tantric sex with an Asian sex master? This was the opportunity of a lifetime, and she ought to be giddy with excitement, not wrapped up in a bundle of anxiety. It had been two years since Marty. Longer still since the physical side had been good, if ever. What if she couldn't perform? What if she didn't do the Tantric stuff right? What if, at the end of it all, Stephen looked at her as though she was dried mud on his Italian shoes?

She glanced to her right. He walked through the lobby as if he owned it. Everyone noticed him and dipped their heads in acknowledgment, as if greeting royalty. It was just that commanding air he had. What the hell was she doing here? Any minute now, someone was going to point a finger at her and scream: punked!

But no one did. And within moments, they were in the elevator. She tensed. She couldn't help it. Marty had thought it great fun to paw at her whenever they were alone in an elevator like this. He hadn't cared if there were video cameras or that the doors might open and show her disheveled self to anyone. In fact, he loved it when someone smirked at them, knowing what they'd been doing.

But Stephen did nothing. He merely stood there, like a remote Chinese god—excruciatingly polite, exquisitely handsome, and absolutely not trying to get his hand into her pants. She didn't know if she was relieved or disappointed.

Her eyes dropped lower. His pants were perfectly tailored and somewhat generous in certain areas. But her ego was pleased to notice that he wasn't unaffected by her. That was something at least. She wasn't the only one standing around aching in places that hadn't ached in a really long time. She wanted him bad. Her whole body felt wet and hungry despite the nerves.

"Tell me about Hong Kong," she suddenly said. Then she bit her lip and cursed herself for being stupid. She'd just neatly pointed out how very small-town she was, how untraveled and inexperienced. Why not just write Backwoods Hick on her forehead?

But he didn't roll his eyes at her. Instead, he tilted his head and stared off into the distance. One dark lock of his black hair had slipped across his forehead, nearly into his eyes. Everything about him was so perfect, it was nice to see something that wasn't exactly where it ought to be.

"Hong Kong is tall and crowded. The best and the worst of everything can be bought there, and everywhere people are scrambling for money—a penny, a ruble, a yuan, it matters not. They can be equally bloodthirsty over a carved piece of ugly rock or an exquisite tiara of diamonds."

"And you love it." She could hear the affection in his voice.

He smiled. "That's such an American concept—loving the place of your birth. Hong Kong is what it is. I live there, and so I endeavor to thrive there."

The elevator dinged and the doors opened. At his gesture she stepped out and they walked down the hallway to his suite. He stood beside her, his arm extended behind her back without touching. As if he escorted but didn't want to push. Either way, she slowed as she turned back to him.

"I think you're lying."

He pulled back, obviously startled. "I don't understand."

"You talk like Hong Kong is just a place, but there is warmth in your voice and a…a dreaminess in your expression. It's not just American to love the land of your birth. Are you saying you don't have any national pride?"

He tilted his head. "Of course I love my country. China is a great land and a great people!" He sounded as if he were reciting propaganda slogans. "But you asked about Hong Kong."

In her mind, China and Hong Kong were one and the

same, but of course they weren't. Until 1997, Hong Kong had been British, and from what she'd heard, it was a teeming capitalist society far different from the mainland. She shook her head. The complexities of politics could be fascinating, but that's not what she was interested in at the moment.

"What do you *feel* when you think of Hong Kong?" She didn't know why she was pressing this point. She just wanted to know him more as a man before they hopped into bed. Sure, she'd been ready for anything on the couch, but that had been twenty minutes ago. Now she was standing in the hallway of a hotel feeling awkward and self-conscious.

His brows narrowed but not in condemnation. He was thinking. "I feel for people, Zoe. Affection or disgust, challenge or lust. Most especially lust." His eyes darkened with promise, and she knew he was talking about his desire for her. "But I do not feel for a city. It is merely a collection of souls crammed together feeling their own lusts."

She noticed that he said nothing of love. No doubt he would call that an American concept as well. Meanwhile, he opened the door to his suite, flicked on the light and gestured her inside. "Would you like me to order food or wine, perhaps? Whatever you need to make you more comfortable."

She shook her head. She didn't think she could eat right now, and the only thing that would make her more comfortable was if he stopped being so...so foreign. She bit her lip. "Maybe this isn't a good idea."

He sighed. It was a purely masculine sound of frustration and it abruptly made him seem human. Species: human male. She smiled.

"Teasing!" she lied, and she slipped into his room before she could change her mind. She was starting to feel more comfortable with him, and she was *not* going to lose this opportunity because of nerves. Then she turned around to find him staring at her with a bizarre mixture of shock and confusion—also very male—and the sight relaxed her enough to make her smile. "Okay, now you seem completely human."

He frowned. "As opposed to turtle or dog?"

"Does it feed your ego too much if I say godlike?"

He raised his eyebrows. "Definitely not. Feel free to call me godlike at any time."

"Yeah, thought so. I..." Her words ended on a sigh as he touched her face, caressing it in a long stroke that made her shiver.

"I have been waiting too long to get you alone," he said.

She swallowed and consciously let her spine relax until she molded herself against his lean body. "Definitely human male," she murmured. Then she looked at his mouth, unable to stop herself from saying the first thing that came to mind. "Is it time to start kissing again?"

He smiled, his lips lengthening in a purely male and also rather Cheshire-cat-like motion. "Kissing is an excellent way to start your energies flowing."

Her energies were flowing. She was sure of it. But she didn't say that. Instead, she lifted her chin. "I have been practicing the breast circles, opening up the energy gate there."

He raised his eyebrows. "Then we can proceed directly to making the power flow." He spent another long moment looking at her face, most especially her mouth. And then...then...then he stepped back.

She blinked, feeling abruptly bereft. "Stephen?"

He walked away from her, shedding his jacket and dimming the lights in quick movements. He turned up the heat and walked into the bedroom, whipping all the covers off the bed with one mighty heave. All that remained was a great big expanse of white cotton. Then he started pulling off his shirt.

"I have only the barest supplies here. I apologize. I had to pack quickly." He flipped open a small suitcase. She had to take a tiny step into his bedroom to see what was inside it. And when she did, she blinked. Lotions, candles, incense and…toys? Carved ivory sex toys? Not to mention feathers, studded leather and sandpaper.

Meanwhile, Stephen continued to work. His shirt was off, but he kept his pants on, sans belt. And he'd kicked off his shoes, so he moved about the room silently as he struck tiny matches and lit a half dozen beeswax candles. She could tell that they were arranged according to some ritual because he was acting as solemnly as a monk at an altar. That and because he messed up, mixing the order of two of them and then had to blow out the candles and relight them correctly.

An exotic fragrance filled the air. She might have been able to identify the scents individually, but blended like this, they just became a blur of Asian smells. Erotic Asian smells, since his erection seemed to grow larger and larger as he moved about the room. Clearly this was a well-practiced response. Light the candles, gonna have sex. Guys were Pavlovian.

And so, apparently, was she. Because just the sight of the light glistening off the smooth planes of his chest made her grow wet and willing. She didn't want to think she was that easy, but he was one potent package despite the weirdness of the situation and his sex kit. Just so long as he didn't reach for that sandpaper, she was likely to go anywhere he led.

When he finished, he turned to look at her hovering in the doorway. His expression was calm and completely focused. As if he was gearing up to climb a mountain or run a 10K. Then he smiled. Damn, he was a pretty, pretty man. Hollywood made smiles like that into superstars.

"Do not be afraid," he said softly.

Said the spider to the fly?

"This is not about sex," he continued. "This is about energy. About raising your energy to its highest peak."

She nodded because…well, what else was she going to do? After all, she'd chosen this. She *wanted* to do this. It was just so…unfamiliar.

"Why don't we begin with the familiar? Come, sit on the bed and do your breast circles."

Right. Breast circles. She'd done them daily for a while now. She'd even done them in a class with Tracy and in front of Nathan. How much different could it be with Stephen?

A lot different, apparently. Months ago, she had blithely stripped off her crop top to bare her breasts. Now she sat on the edge of Stephen's bed and couldn't manage to grip the base of her sweatshirt. Her palms were sweaty and she couldn't catch her breath. How would she ever find the calm she needed—

Her thoughts skittered to a frozen halt when she felt his hand on her shoulder. She couldn't even turn her head to look at him, but he moved closer, sliding his hand across her back until he had to crawl up on the bed behind her.

"W-what are you doing?" she stammered.

"Shhh," he said against her hair. "I'm just going to hold you. That's all."

"I suppose the women you're used to aren't this skittish, huh?" she said with a laugh. Or at least she tried for a laugh. It came out more like a sick wheeze.

"You'd be surprised," he drawled. "And no reaction is wrong so long as it is honest."

"Bad juju to lie to your partner?" she asked.

He paused. Probably didn't understand the word *juju*. Then she felt his hands tighten for a moment as he squeezed her upper arms. "Bad to lie to me, definitely. Much, much worse to lie to yourself."

It sounded as though he had some experience in both, but she didn't have time to explore further. He was settling behind her, his knees bracketing her hips, his hands sliding all the way down to her fingers. His breath heated the back of her neck, and she shivered at the feel of her hair shifting with his exhalations.

"You surround me," she whispered.

He froze. "Too much?"

She shook her head, letting her eyes close to better enjoy the moment. "Once, I would have hated it. Too much weight, too much restriction."

"And now?"

"It's nice to lean on someone, if only for a moment."

"I am very strong," he said, and she could hear the smile in his words. "Lean on me as long as you like. I swear to release you whenever you wish to go."

She hardly thought that would happen. He was likely to tire of her long before she wanted to leave him. But she didn't say that. Instead, she took a deep breath, and focused on being present in her body. She sat with her back to his naked front, his heat making her breath short. His arms wrapped around her, lightly touching her upper arms. She shifted her position out of nervousness, then was startled to realize she hadn't bumped into him. He was mirroring her actions, as if he knew how she would move before she did.

She grinned. He really was a gentleman. The thought was novel enough that she barely noticed when she pulled off her sweatshirt and cami in one motion. She knew she was doing it, of course, but she didn't focus her thoughts on that. Instead, she filled her mind with the fantasy—now reality—that she was about to make love with a prince. And he *was* a prince in her book. Any captain of industry was royalty. Certainly when compared to her or anyone else she knew.

Her upper body was bare now. Her breasts weren't large enough to merit a full underwire contraption. Just the cami that was now somewhere on the bed. He still held her, and she allowed her back to touch his chest— skin to skin—and the heat of him seared into her spine.

She didn't move. She couldn't. Not while she was consumed by the heat of him. Except her hands apparently were disconnected from her failing mind. They knew the patterns of the breast circles and began them all on their own. Starting at the outside of her nipples, she began stroking a widening circle around and around her breasts as a way of dispersing negative energy. His hands moved with hers, touching the backs of her fingers lightly with his own. He didn't add weight, barely even added sensation because he moved in concert with her. But she felt him as if he were the one stroking her.

"You have been doing this for a while," he murmured against her ear. "I can feel how clear your energy is."

"Liar," she murmured. She felt anything but clear right then.

"No," he said, and his word had the strength of a vow. "I never lie to my partner. Ever."

She didn't know how to respond to that, so she kept silent. She simply allowed her hands to flow around her breasts while he shadowed her every movement, every breath. Yes, she realized with shock, he was even breathing in tandem with her.

"Forty-nine," she whispered as her hands came to rest at the base of her rib cage. She didn't truly know if she had circled her breasts forty-nine times, but it felt as though she had. They felt cool and clean, as if she had been bathing in a clear mountain stream.

"May I perform the energizing strokes?" he asked. There was no pressure in the question. He might have been asking her to pass the salt. But he wanted to touch her breasts, and she was nearly weak with the need for him to do exactly that.

"Please," she said, her voice coming out a hoarse croak. She let her hands drop away, only to be replaced by the pads of three large fingers pressed just beneath each breast.

"Lean back against me," he said. "Relax and breathe with my stroke. Allow the energy to flow out of you and into my hands. In this way…"

"…we will link as partners." She'd read that in one of the Tantric texts. She closed her eyes and tried to steady her breathing. Odd that she wasn't panting. Her inhalations and exhalations were steady, smooth movements.

"Don't control anything, Zoe, most especially your breath. That's how I will know the state of your excitement."

She twisted slightly to look at him. "I thought you would feel the energy."

He flashed her a rakish smile. "Well, that, too." Then he sobered a bit. "Normally, these circles are done with the heel of your foot—"

"Pressed to my groin, yes. I remember." She felt her face heat to scarlet. Here she was sitting with his hands on her breasts, and she was embarrassed about pulling off her pants?

"If you want, you could simply unbutton your jeans. That will give you more freedom of movement and allow you to stroke yourself if you so choose."

She blinked. "You want me to... I should... By myself?" In front of him?

"Only if you want. It is merely a suggestion. It is only that I know that jeans can feel rather restrictive." There was a dry note to his voice that made her wonder if he was experiencing the same problem himself.

And so to help him, she shyly flicked open the button of her jeans and tugged the zipper down. "Feel, um, free to do so yourself," she said as she worked.

"Thank you. I will." But he didn't move his hands. "Are you ready?"

She steadied herself. Truthfully it did feel much better to have her pants undone but not off. And there was a reassurance, too, that he had *not* undone his pants. She felt the smooth material against her lower back, and the hot bulge beneath. Hot and hard and so very there, but muted by the fabric, for which she was grateful.

Then his hands began to move. They flowed easily around her breasts, pressing only slightly in her skin, brushing in tighter and tighter circles until his fingers ended at the side of her nipples. So close, but never quite touching the tips. Then he stopped and repositioned his hands beneath her breasts.

The motion was smooth. He had obviously done it before to other women. Maybe hundreds of other women, but the thought disappeared as soon as it formed. He was here with her now, and now was oh so much more interesting than some imagined previous harem.

Her breasts were swelling, becoming hot and full as the energy built. She had felt this before, of course, but never this fast and never this hot. An inferno blazed just beneath her skin, and it was growing. Her head dropped back onto his shoulder as she tried to simultaneously cool her neck and lift her breasts to a deeper caress.

"You have such yin power," he murmured. "It presses against me like the sun."

Flatterer, she thought, but couldn't find the breath to voice the word. And once again, the negative thought faded away beneath the power of the present moment. It did feel as if she had twin suns blazing behind each breast.

"I am going to open the lesser yin gate now. Do not be afraid."

She wasn't so long as he kept stroking her. His hands circled her breasts again, this time using four fingers. The fire blazed where he touched and lingered well after he moved on. She could barely keep track of his position and soon gave up trying. If only he would touch her nipples. If only he would…

He tugged, a sharp pull on both sides at once. A brilliant flash of sensation ripped through her consciousness. Like a solar flare, it burned then faded, but the memory lingered in her gasping breath. He returned to stroke around her breasts again, pulling energy from the outside in as he spiraled upward.

Zoe held her breath. Her breasts felt huge, as though they had expanded to include her entire body. And his hands circled and stroked every part of her. Then he paused and she nearly cried out at the interruption.

"Don't hold your breath, Zoe. Breath makes the fire hotter. Breath makes the energy flow. Breath…"

"…is life," she said, and for once the words didn't sound corny. When she breathed in time with his strokes, it helped everything in her expand.

"Life," he echoed, then he shifted backward. He continued to stroke her, but he was moving her to lie down on the bed. She didn't know how he accomplished it. She never felt as if he'd abandoned her body as she stretched out. But maybe that was Stephen's power. That he could touch her without physically contacting her. She didn't know and she didn't want to spoil the illusion by looking. So she simply lay down, allowing her legs and her arms to flop open.

And still the strokes continued, flowing upward over her breasts, around and around until she felt that gloriously wonderful tug on her nipples. Each time the pull grew stronger and deeper, as if he stroked a molten hot cord that burned from nipple to core. She felt the tug in her spine, too, up in her brain and all the way down to her womb. Most especially her womb.

Was it possible to orgasm from breast circles? She thought so, but never would she have believed it if she weren't lying here while Stephen caressed her breasts to white hot suns of yin power.

Then he squeezed both her nipples again in a long pulling grip. It was almost painful or perhaps just painful enough, and she cried out, arching her back.

"Not enough," he said. "It's not enough."

It felt like enough. It felt like oceans of enough, and yet she wanted more. "How?" she gasped. She didn't have the coherence to say anything else. And then she knew. That's why he'd asked her to unbutton her pants.

Her hands felt incredibly weak but she managed to link her thumbs in her waistband and shove them down. She got her jeans off her hips, but not her panties, and she let out a little mew of distress.

Thankfully, he understood what she wanted. She felt him shift off the bed and tug her pants away. He even touched her as reverently as if she were a princess. It was sweet of him, and she adored him for it, but she was impatient. She wanted his hands on her now.

"Stroke your breasts, Zoe," he instructed from her knees. "Keep the fire hot while I try to get the energy flowing here."

Here? Where? She felt his fingers burning hot as he made fluttering strokes down her ribs and then deeper down her belly. Oh! she realized. There!

Her panties were white cotton hip-huggers, worn thin from age and now soaking wet. He peeled them down and it felt as if he were slowly pulling the skin off a ripe peach. She almost giggled at the thought of herself as a peach, but the sensation was so real.

"Touch me," she cried. "Oh, please touch me!" She had never felt this hot before.

His hands were between her knees, gently pushing them apart. Then he lifted her legs up and over to settle on his shoulders. Her feet dangled uselessly down his back, and her inner core blazed from the touch of cool air.

"Keep stroking your breasts, Zoe!"

She was. She couldn't stop herself. But that wasn't where her attention was centered. The heat was burning down her spine and building up in her womb. She whimpered. She needed something, but her mind couldn't grasp what. She just needed.

"Now we can begin for real," he said as he spread her even farther. Then he kissed her in the most intimate of places. Deep and long and with a tongue that swirled and probed and pushed. Around and in, over and in, around and over, around and over, and in and in and…

"Yes!"

5

SWEET HEAVEN, she was a miracle! Stephen pressed his mouth to the wonderful Zoe and drank her yin energy like a starving man. But it was like taking gulps beneath a rushing river. There was so much and it was all so sweet! Never had he thought to feel such purity, such amazing power, and it all came from Zoe, the girl he had initially dismissed. How wrong he had been! And how arrogant!

She was still flowing! He drank and drank and could not get enough.

"Stop! Oh, you've got to stop!" she gasped. She was struggling weakly against him, trying to close her legs, to pull him away, but he didn't want it to end. Just remembering this moment would stiffen his dragon organ for years to come.

"Stephen! Please! I can't…I can't!" She scooted backward, away from him.

He could have kept her still. He was much stronger than she, even without the orgasm still coursing through her body. If she were more mature in the practice, he probably would have. Old tigresses strove endlessly for a torrent such as Zoe was still producing. But she was young, and if he felt a bit overwhelmed, she must be completely buried beneath the tide. So he let her go and watched as she rolled onto her side and…and…started crying?

He pushed up from the side of the bed, though his legs were unsteady. Poor thing. It had been too much for her mind. A whole torrent of emotions often flooded the novices during the smallest of yin flows. This had been a deluge. Who knew what feelings she was struggling with?

"Zoe?" he said softly. "Don't cry. It'll get better, I promise. The first time is always hard…"

Her chest started heaving, and he felt an unexpected awkwardness. This was why he never trained novices. Everything was so unpredictable with them. But he couldn't abandon her. She needed him now, and so he reached out and stroked her arm.

"Just breathe, Zoe. Focus on your breath, nothing else. The emotion will pass—"

She flopped onto her back, and he saw tears streaming from her eyes. He felt a moment of painful sympathy until he realized that she wasn't crying with unhappiness. No, she was…laughing? Laughing so hard that tears flowed almost as fast as her yin river.

"Oh, my God," he whispered. "Your mind is broken. Oh, Zoe, I'm so sorry."

There was a moment's hitch in her breath, and then she clutched her belly as big gasping laughter rolled out of her. "Oh," she cried. "Oh, that hurts. Oh! Oh!"

He could almost think she was orgasming again, but one look at her body and he could tell that the afterglow was simply that: afterglow. But just to make sure, he reached out his hand and tried to touch her with all his senses. Closing his eyes, he felt tingling joy shimmering against his fingertips. She was still bubbling over with yin, and it was making her laugh.

He smiled, pleased that he had brought her to such a

glorious place. And a little jealous, too. Women had it so much easier in this practice than men.

He opened his eyes, letting his hand fall to the sheets beside her. Her fair skin had flushed to a blotchy red, and yet he found the whole package infinitely beautiful. Pure yin could not fail to be glorious, and so he decided to catch a little more of it.

She had rolled half onto her side, giggling in sporadic bursts, so he spooned in beside her, allowing her energy to bathe him from head to toe. "You are incredible," he murmured as he pressed his mouth to the back of her neck. There was a chakra point there, and he could suck some more yin from her.

She shivered against him, and his organ reacted painfully to the jostling. "Is it always like that?" she asked.

He reluctantly lifted his mouth off her chakra point. "Like what? You will have to describe what happened for me to know."

"Like rainbows and waterfalls," she whispered. "Like an infinite expanse of…of…shimmering. That's the word. It was like the whole world shimmered."

He straightened, lifting his head as he looked down at her. "You…shimmered?"

"Yes," she whispered. "Like a zillion points of light all tingly and, oh…wow, it was glorious."

He frowned. Had she really climbed to heaven on her first try? Then another thought followed quickly behind the first: he was good. She might be a natural, but he had brought it out in her. That was an accomplishment to be proud of. He need not feel jealous of her experience, simply pleased that he had helped her attain it.

"That is most excellent," he said smoothly, making

sure none of his thoughts were revealed on his face. "That bodes well for our partnership. Congratulations."

Her body was still trembling, her breath still unsteady. He couldn't stop himself from pressing his hand to her back just to feel the aftershocks. "Tell me," he begged. "Tell me what you felt."

She sighed and rolled to her back. His hand slipped from her spine, around her rib cage, to settle on her stomach just below her breasts. She didn't even seem to notice. Her eyes were still focused on that far-off place he couldn't see. And she didn't say one damn thing.

So he leaned forward, taking her pebbled nipple into his mouth. He rolled it with his tongue, nipping and pulling in the way he had been trained. She shuddered beneath him and moaned.

"No, Stephen. Wow, no more." She pushed weakly at his shoulder, but he refused to stop. If only in this small way, he needed to lap up all of her experience he could. If she wouldn't talk, then he would take her overflow yin.

He redoubled his efforts. She groaned, but his mouth didn't tingle yet from her yin. He began to suck.

"Oh, stop!" she cried, abruptly pushing him away. The force of her shove made him release her with a pop. And when he looked at her face, he saw a flushed anger. Then, while he waited, she took a breath. "Look, I know, I know. It's been all about me, and you want your turn. I know. Just…please, give me a minute, okay? Please?"

He frowned at her. "I don't understand."

She blinked, and her voice betrayed her irritation. "You don't understand giving me a moment to recover? To savor the afterglow? Come on, Stephen, it can't be all about you all the time. Just give me a moment!"

He buttoned his lips. Clearly, that was what she wanted, but he didn't understand why. She wanted to be left alone, probably to meditate. He understood the need to process an otherworldly experience, so he dipped his head and rolled off the bed. He would get his e-mail. Though if anything was guaranteed to darken his mood, it was his e-mail.

He stood up, taking a moment to relish the full weight of his organ. He breathed deeply, focusing on the power he had absorbed and the way it flowed through his body and concentrated in his groin. Such purity. Such power. Surely he would be able to make his own ascent to the heavenly realm with her energy.

Meanwhile, he heard Zoe release a sigh of disgust. Was he lingering in the room too long? He bowed out without even grabbing his shirt, barely having time to fasten his pants. Then he left the room, shutting the door as silently as possible. He went to his computer with his own sigh of disgust.

Sure enough, a few keystrokes later and he was looking at e-mail from his EVP Shen Jiao Kai. The weight of his responsibilities came crashing down, and even Zoe's power wasn't proof against the problems that faced him on his electronic screen. His company had overextended. Then the world economic crisis had hit, and everything he owned was now on the verge of collapse. He dropped his chin into his hand and stared, his mind churning with problems that had no easy solution.

"What, you don't get what you need, so you leave? Isn't that like a little boy?"

He turned, his eyes once again drinking in the sight of her. She'd pulled on the hotel robe, and it dwarfed her, but he still remembered the petite body underneath. "Have you recovered?" he asked, doing his best not to react to her tone. She was angry at him, and he really didn't understand why. "Were you able to successfully meditate?"

She stared at him, and her expression shifted into perplexed. "I get the feeling that we're having two entirely different conversations. Am I getting angry here for the absolutely wrong reasons?"

He shook his head. "Many women become surly when they return from the heavenly realm. It is because they have no wish to return to the present world. So they become angry."

"And take out that anger on their partners? That's a bit unfair, don't you think?"

He shrugged. "Emotions are not fair. They simply are. I have experienced enough tigress attacks not to take it personally."

She folded her arms. "Then you're a better person than I am." She abruptly crossed to the chair nearest his desk, dropping down into it with the casualness of so many American women. He found the honesty of the movement refreshing and smiled. "But that wasn't why I was annoyed. I thought you were impatient for your turn." She swallowed. "Marty—my ex—wouldn't ever let me just be, you know? Rest and enjoy? It was always about him. So I just assumed you were being like him." She bit her lip and sighed. "That was unfair of me because you are obviously not like him."

He raised his eyebrows. "I enjoyed myself thoroughly, Zoe. I drank your yin until I was bursting."

She frowned. "So I had no reason to be annoyed at all. I'm so sorry." She glanced behind her at the bedroom. "So did you want to go back and…um…get your turn?"

He shook his head. "I had my turn." He flashed her a warm smile. "It was wonderful. Thank you."

"Uh, you're welcome, I think." She kept looking at him as though he was insane. "But you don't want to, you know, keep going?"

"You wish to absorb some of my yang? I can accommodate you now, if you like. I have worked extrahard to purify my semen emissions, but I don't know if it will come close to what you have given me."

This time she was the one who didn't speak, but just stared. It took him a moment to figure out why.

"Oh," he abruptly realized. "I forget that you know nothing of our temple in Hong Kong or the regimen there. Here." He quickly tapped some keys and the printer began spitting out the file. When it was done, he passed it to her.

"What's this?" she asked as she flipped through the four-page document.

"It is my schedule. As you can see, the herbs are most carefully regulated for clarity. I have tried a variety of different combinations over the years. I began, as most do, trying to increase potency. But after many years, I find that it does me little good anymore. I then began experimenting for taste and volume. But truly, I think clarity seems to be the best choice now."

She nodded, her eyes very wide. "This is a regimen for your semen…um…potency?"

He nodded. "Of course."

"And you've worked for potency, taste and volume, but now you think you need to work on clarity."

He leaned forward and directed her attention to the third page. "I, of course, do regular exercises to maintain what levels I have already achieved. I just found that further attention yielded no increases beyond my current levels."

"Ah," she drawled, and he detected a note of sarcasm. "So you've peaked in those areas and therefore directed your attention to…um…clarity. What exactly does that mean?"

"My semen is nearly at optimal opalescence. It has a pearly white color that borders on translucence." He tapped another key and pulled up his graphic on his progress in all the key areas. They were coded by date and any objective means of evaluation that he could find. "If you like, I can e-mail these to you for further study."

She shook her head. "No, really, that's okay."

He looked at her, comprehension slowly dawning. With a careful movement, he shut his laptop and turned toward her. "You find all of this bizarre."

She bit her lip and looked guilty. "Um, yeah. A little."

"I thought you had read all the texts Nathan gave you."

She nodded. "Most of them."

"Did you read the ones from Ancient China? The texts from the Yellow Emperor are most—"

"I thought they were…um…legend. I thought a modern man wouldn't ever…"

"You thought that I would not follow the dictates of the practice? The Tigress Mother herself recommends this course to all male students. I take ascension seriously enough to do all that was dictated by the Yellow Emperor."

She flushed and looked down at her hands. "Well, it is rather…um…a lot."

He sighed. "So you are a dabbler, after all."

Her eyes widened in shock. "What? No! I mean—"

"I know what you meant," he said softly. "It is what often happens with the beginners. It is a wonderful practice and quite fun to experience orgasms without end. But once you are required to do more than enjoy, once it takes thought and meditation and a regimen of herbs, all the dabblers fall away. They cannot imagine working so hard for something so natural as sex."

She flushed scarlet. "But sex *is* natural," she said softly.

"Not the sex that takes one's spirit to heaven. How is it that you could attain such heights without even understanding the basics?" He felt the acrid taste of bitterness in his throat and consciously softened his tone. "I am being surly. I apologize. I shouldn't take my envy out on you."

She looked back up at him, her eyes startled. "Envy?"

Her confusion actually made him smile. "You truly have no idea how amazing you are." He leaned forward, touching her hands. "You felt heaven this night. That shimmering was the edges of the lowest levels of heaven. It took me many years to get there. And a great deal of herbs and meditations."

"To heaven," she said, her eyes on his printed pages. "I thought this was a way of purifying one's energies to attain greater—"

"Heaven, Zoe. To attain heaven."

She nodded, but her expression still showed confusion. "But isn't that a metaphorical kind of heaven?"

He tilted his head. "Did that last experience feel metaphorical? Were your shimmers symbolic or real?"

"Real," she whispered. "Very, very real."

He raised an eyebrow, waiting for her to travel the rest of the logic path.

"So all that stuff—Chamber of a Thousand Swinging Lanterns, heavenly gates and angels—those are all real?"

He nodded. "At least the Chamber is. I haven't gone beyond that level for many years now."

"A room with swinging lights."

"And so much more." He said the words calmly, but his heart had sunk to his toes. She was so talented, and yet she obviously didn't believe in any of this. If only she would open up her mind! He wanted to touch her, to press the truth into her skin in a very physical way, but he knew better than to try. So he leaned back and folded his arms to keep himself apart from her.

"There is really only one question here, Zoe. Do you believe that you could purify your energies to such clarity that your spirit wanders through a real heaven? A place of angels and pearly gates and such wonder as you cannot even imagine?"

She frowned. "And by purify, you mean through sex? And herbs and stuff."

"The body reflects the soul, doesn't it?"

She nodded, but he could tell she wasn't convinced. "But it's just sex," she murmured, then she bit her lip. "Don't get angry…" She hesitated. "But why do you believe this? Doesn't it sound a bit…well, far-fetched?"

"I am not angry," he bit out. But he was. He had so wanted to explore this with her. She had such power, and yet it was all wasted because she didn't believe. "Your friend Tracy has gone to the Chamber of a Thousand Swinging Lanterns. You yourself shimmered on your first try. And yet you sit there refusing to believe."

She shrugged. "Tracy and I aren't really that close. We've talked and all, but I only know her because she's with Nathan, who's my teacher. Or was my teacher…" Her voice trailed away. She was speaking randomly to cover her confusion.

He turned away. He'd thought he'd at last found the right partner, a woman of natural purity and an honest, open heart. That's what he'd felt when he kissed her. That's how pure her energies were. But she didn't believe. So there could be no progress until she accepted the purpose of their practice.

"Stephen…" she began, but no words followed. She didn't know what to say.

"I do not fault you for your choices, Zoe." Then he abruptly straightened, noting with disgust that his dragon organ had withered to nothing. Even her yin power had been an illusion. "This happens all the time, Zoe. Partners have different goals. I am sorry it didn't work out between us, but we tried." He pulled out his wallet and handed her a twenty-dollar bill. "I hope this will cover your cab fare—"

"You don't need to—"

"Don't argue. I can more than afford it." He glanced significantly at the time. "It is midday in Hong Kong, and I have pressing business matters. Please forgive me for not walking you to the door."

She huffed. "Of course you don't have to walk me to the door. But I want to make amends—"

"There is no need. Nothing to apologize for. We attempted a partnership, it did not work. There is no shame in that."

"You sound like my divorce lawyer," she drawled.

"Then he is a wise man."

"Not really."

He didn't pull back his hand until she reluctantly took the money from him. "Did you want any food or anything?" he offered. "Something before you go?"

"No," she said softly. "I don't need anything else. And I won't bother you any longer."

She turned away, and he thought he caught a glimpse

of tears in her eyes. Guilt ate him, but what could he have done differently? While she dressed, he popped open his laptop and pretended to work. But his attention was focused on her, on the whispers of movement as she pulled on her clothes. On the soft gasps of breath as she tried to control her emotions. On every aspect of her presence in his hotel room as she disturbed his peace and confused his emotions.

Why would he feel bad about her leaving? She was exactly what he had feared: a dabbler only interested in a great night—or week—of weird sex. People like that were everywhere in this practice. It was no tragedy, though he was saddened that she clearly thought him insane. Well, she wasn't the first, nor would she be the last.

He sighed, trying to focus on his failing business. Jiao Kai had sent him statistics on the pork-packaging plant. The numbers did not look good.

Zoe was dressed now. She had collected her things and was hovering uncertainly behind him. He turned to face her. "If you wait a moment, I'll get dressed. I can stand with you while you wait for the cab."

"No!" she practically cried. "No, no. I wouldn't dream of bothering you further."

"I don't mind," he said softly. It wasn't a lie. Though he had no clue why he would want to stretch this awful goodbye out even longer.

"No," she said firmly. "I'm a big girl. I just wanted to say thank you. I had a really good time. And I'm sorry I didn't understand this right."

He shrugged. "You have repaid me in yin." Illusionary yin, but it had been glorious nonetheless. "I am most grateful for that." Then he stood up, needing to touch her one last time. He allowed himself a quick stroke of her cheek. "If you change your mind… If you choose to study further, then please contact me."

"You'd still partner with me?"

Yes! his irrational heart cried. But his mind stepped in with a long list of practicalities. In the end, he sighed. "I live in Hong Kong most of the year. We will try to find you a partner where you live."

"Of course. I understand."

He headed for the bedroom. "Let me get on a shirt."

"No," she said. "Don't." Then, while he had one arm inside a sweater, she rushed out the door. He watched the door click shut behind her and debated whether he should run after her. For what? To stand there awkwardly while she called for a cab? What would he say to her? He had no idea. Just as he had no idea why he had such a strong urge to stay with her.

It was because he didn't want to face his business problems, he decided. It had nothing to do with Zoe and everything to do with the disaster waiting for him on the other side of the globe. Therefore, the only mature response was to sit back down at his computer and return to work. He needed to sit down, forget Zoe, and carefully study the pork packager's monthly reports.

So that was exactly what he did. And then did again. And again. In fact, he had to redo, refocus and rediscipline himself at least seventeen times that night before finally giving up and going to bed. A bed where she had lain, where she had climaxed, where he had drunk such sweet yin…

He groaned and buried his face in a pillow she had *not* used. It didn't help.

6

ZOE WAS DROPPING with fatigue after working the 4:00 a.m. shift at the Bread Café, then attending classes. She had meant to go to speak with Stephen, but was just too exhausted to try. Or maybe it wasn't exhaustion so much as depression. She felt like a major heel after last night. After all, she had been the one begging to find a partner. She just hadn't expected that anyone took the rigors of the practice *that* seriously. Charts and herbs, exercises and who knew what else!

But she got the feeling that Stephen took everything seriously. Sure, the man could be charming and had a smile to end all smiles, but it only seemed to go skin-deep. She had the feeling that beneath all that charm was a very sad little boy.

She could picture him now, a dark-haired child with a somber expression. In her imagination, she didn't ask questions. She simply opened her arms to him and let him dash against her. He was angry at first, but eventually, the little boy in her mind tucked a fist tight to his chin and buried his face against her chest as she lay down on the bed. Then together they slept.

She woke late in the afternoon with Janet banging on her door. "Zoe! Zoe! *He's* here!"

"Coming!" she called as she pushed away the pillow

she had been cuddling in her sleep. In her mind's eye, she kissed the sleeping boy on his forehead. It was stupid, but all she had these days was her fantasy life, so she would hold to it despite all logic. Then she pulled a brush through her hair and rushed downstairs.

She made it to the first floor and zipped around the corner, her heart beating triple-time as she looked for the grown-up version of the little boy she'd been snuggling in her sleep. He wasn't there. Not in the main room, that is.

"Hello?" she called.

"Back here!" came a voice from the kitchen.

She rushed to the back of the house only to stop cold a foot inside the kitchen door. She'd been looking for a tall Chinese aristocrat. What she found instead was matted sandy hair and the greasy face of her ex-husband. She bit her lip, the disappointment keen.

"Marty, get out."

"Uh-uh." He was chewing a cheeseburger and shaking his head. Then he gestured to his fries, and she hated that her mouth actually watered. Hell, she was human. She could like French fries, just not the jerk offering them.

"Get out, Marty." She held open the door to the kitchen.

Janet and Rachel burst into the room. Rachel swam for the university swim team and had the shoulders to prove it. She looked very buff in her sweats and stretchy tank, perfectly designed to outline her weight-lifter muscles. Janet's ponytail flopped about her shoulders in her agitation.

"He just waved his burger at me and headed to the kitchen!" Janet huffed.

Rachel folded her arms, biceps bulging. "Get out now or Janet'll call the cops while I *throw* your thieving ass out."

Marty visibly paled, but he shoved his hand into his pocket and pulled out a few wadded bills. "I didn't take your Visa gift card, Zoe, but I figured I'd help you out with what I got." He pressed the bills into her hand.

Zoe wanted to throw the crumpled money back into his face, but it was the most she was likely to see from the bastard, so she quickly straightened the bills. "Forty-seven dollars. Gee, thanks," she drawled. "Especially since you stole four hundred."

"I didn't steal anything! And you got no cause to be calling the cops on me, harassing me at work."

Her eyebrows rose in surprise. "You got a job?"

He nodded. "At the bowling alley. Your mom set it up."

"Wasn't that nice of her. But you still owe me the four hundred bucks you stole, not to mention the eight hundred fifty you borrowed to get your truck fixed."

He shook his head, then lifted his burger for another big bite. "You gave me that money fair and square."

"No, you forged my signature on my credit card, then sweet-talked me into not siccing the cops on you. But you promised to pay me back. That was three months ago, so now…" She did a swift calculation in her head. "You now owe me just over nine hundred dollars for the car—"

"What!"

"Interest, sweet cheeks. If I get charged interest, then so do you. Plus four hundred for the gift card."

"I didn't take any damn gift card!"

"Then how'd you know it was a Visa gift card and not a check? Or cash?"

He frowned. "The cops said."

"No, they didn't. They wouldn't." It was a lie. She had no idea what they'd said to Marty and what they hadn't.

It didn't matter. They all knew her sleazy ex had taken the money. God, what had she ever seen in the guy?

Meanwhile, Marty was wiping off his mouth and putting on his charming face. "Aw, come on, Zoe, don't be like that. I thought we could hang out at the bowling alley with your parents tonight. It's your dad's league night. We could get some beer. I got employee rates now. It would be like old times."

"Yes," she said with a sigh. "It would. Especially with you *drinking beer,* and all."

He winced. "I don't drink and drive anymore. You know that."

"That's good," she said, "but it's the drinking that's the core problem." It wasn't that Marty was a bad person, but he'd started drinking with his buddies in high school. It had started out with celebration beers after football games, then every Friday night, then throughout the whole weekend. It was just beer, but it was a *lot* of beer. When he'd gotten his first DUI, his coach had told him that his scholarship was in jeopardy. By the third, it was too late. "You're an alcoholic, Marty. You've got to know that."

Marty stiffened. "That's bull, Zoe!"

She sighed. "No, it's not. Maybe you've got it under control right now, maybe you can have one beer and no more, but I don't believe it. You tried that when we were married." And he *had* tried. But then he went back to drinking and started gambling as well. He invested all their money in a copy shop that went belly-up within the first six months. A copy shop!

"I know I screwed up before," he said gently. "But I've changed. The job is real good and I have a shot at being manager in a year."

Zoe rubbed her hand across her face. She'd just

woken up, the damn cheeseburger was making her hungry, and he was looking at her in that way he'd done when they were kids: sweet, charming and with such promise in those baby-blue eyes. They'd had fun back in high school. And she needed some fun these days. But the last thing she needed was to get sucked into Marty's life again. He might be getting it together now, but she had no faith that it would last.

He smiled at her. "You remember the time—"

"Get out." When he opened his mouth to say something else, she waved at her friends. "Go now or the three of us will pin you to the ground and take whatever cash you've got left on you."

His face flattened out into his football grimace. "You wouldn't dare."

"Yeah, I would," growled Rachel.

"Me, too!" piped in Janet.

Marty looked at them and realized they were serious. He cursed and threw his empty burger wrapper at Zoe as he stood up. "When did you become such a bitch?"

"Hmm…maybe it was after your third DUI. Maybe it was when I came home to learn that you'd spent all our money on Copier Heaven. Or maybe when I came here to find my Visa gift card gone. I don't want you in my life, Marty. Go away!"

He left then, making quite a show of how accommodating he was being. Zoe kept up her cold glare. It was easy with Janet and Rachel backing her up. Eventually the door slammed behind his back.

"And good riddance!" Rachel huffed.

Zoe couldn't help but nod. "And to think I believed myself the luckiest girl alive on my wedding day. I guess that goes to show how stupid I was right after high school."

"We all make mistakes," Rachel said, her voice soft with sympathy.

"Yeah, and at least you have that other guy—the Chinese hottie," added Janet.

Zoe sighed, struggled to keep the self-disgust from drowning her. "Actually, I don't think Stephen's coming around again."

Janet frowned. "What happened? He was so into you!"

She shrugged, unwilling to go into details. "I kinda dismissed something he takes very, very seriously."

Rachel flinched. "Oops."

"Yeah. Big oops."

"It wasn't his willy, was it?" Janet asked. "Guys take that really seriously."

Zoe smiled. "No, it wasn't his…um…willy." His willy was definitely not something to laugh at. It was more than adequate for any task. She also realized that except for the time they'd first met when he'd been jet-lagged to the max, Stephen had been nothing but kind to her. From the roses through dinner, then her eternal orgasm, he'd been a perfect gentleman. The idea that she'd been using him to dabble in Tantrism made her feel as low as…well, as if she deserved her thieving user of an ex-husband.

"I've got to make it up to him," she said, thinking out loud. What she planned wasn't going to make up for how she'd acted, but it would be a start. She looked at her friends. "What do you think? Would a Chinese magnate like meatloaf?"

Rachel frowned. "You can't compete with Chinese food. He's gotta be used to the best. And…your meatloaf is the best."

Janet clapped her hands. "It's settled! Meatloaf for dinner!"

"Not so fast." Zoe held up a hand. "Let me see if he'll come first."

She crossed to the house phone and called the hotel. Within moments, she'd gotten him to say yes, though Zoe very much feared she'd taken advantage of him again. He'd sounded as if she'd woken him from a sound sleep, barely coherent as she insisted he come for dinner. She made sure he hadn't scheduled his flight home yet, then said he owed it to her to allow her to apologize.

He muttered something in Chinese at that, but in the end, he agreed. Which meant she had to get busy in the kitchen pronto. And while she cooked, her housemates cleaned. By the time Stephen arrived, everyone was there, all in a tizzy of excitement to check out the Chinese hunk.

He arrived right on time, looking very Bruce Wayne in his black turtleneck and black jeans. His hair had caught some of the snow crystals blowing off the roof from an early frost, and it made him look as if he'd been crowned with diamonds. Janet was the one who opened the door for him, but Rachel made sure Zoe was there to witness his spectacular entrance. Lord, he was a pretty man. He looked like Jet Li dressed to the nines, and her younger and decidedly less cynical housemates practically drooled when he stepped into the foyer.

"Wow." Zoe managed a smile. "You look good. Come on in."

"Thank you," he said. Then he offered her a book. "This is for you."

She took it and wiped the snow off the worn leather binding. "You're not supposed to bring gifts when I'm apologizing to you."

He smiled. "There is no need to apologize, Zoe. We

just have different goals, that's all." Then he gestured to the book, which she now saw was handwritten on pristine linen. "That's an English translation of the scrolls from the Yellow Emperor. It's—"

"That's your handwriting, isn't it? This is your book." Her fingers felt as if they were tingling where they touched the pages. The written words flowed smoothly over the page and notes were scrawled at the side, some in English, some in Chinese.

He smiled. "It was an exercise from my English tutor many years ago. I had to translate something into English."

She raised her eyebrows. "So you chose an ancient Tantric scroll? Wow, what must he have thought?"

Stephen straightened. "That I was an advanced and very mature young man. He said so." Then he flashed her a smile. "He also said that the subject matter accurately reflected the obsessions of my age."

"I'll bet," she said with a laugh. "It's lovely, Stephen, but I can't take this. It's too precious."

"It is nothing of the sort. But if you insist, then return it to me when you are done. At least that way, I can be assured that you contact me again."

She smiled. He wanted to keep in contact with her. That was good. That was very good.

And then, while she stood staring at Stephen, Janet ran out of patience. "Come on, come on, I'm starved! Is dinner ready yet?"

Stephen raised his eyebrows in surprise. "I thought we would be going to a restaurant."

Zoe laughed, surprised that the sound came out light and almost girly. "As my apology to you? I am really sorry, but there's no way I can afford to take you out to dinner. Besides, don't you want a home-cooked meal?"

His expression didn't change. He remained urbane and gracious, though she caught a flash of anxiety in his eyes. "I would enjoy anything you wish to do."

"That's so sweet," Janet cooed. "And don't worry, her meatloaf is to die for. So come on, the kitchen's this way."

Zoe watched his face carefully to see his reaction to meatloaf. There wasn't one. She got the feeling he had locked down all his emotions, determined to suffer through this evening no matter what was in store. She stifled a sigh. She wanted to get to know him better, to share a casual meal with him, not have him sit through an evening as if it were a state dinner of rubber chicken and speeches.

But there was nothing she could do about it now. So she smiled and gestured to the large table in the dining room. Jesse, another of her housemates, had just finished setting out chipped plates and mismatched glasses for seven. Paper napkins from different fast-food restaurants completed the crass display, but it was what they had. At least the cutlery was real instead of plastic.

Jesse gestured to the refrigerator. "Grab a glass and get what you like to drink. Rachel was supposed to serve drinks, but she's on her laptop looking you up. Said she found a gold mine, so be warned."

Zoe tried not to groan. Stephen didn't so much as sigh, but then again, she thought his shoulders had frozen to ice. In fact, an ice sculpture would have had more expression than he did as he turned to her.

"We are to eat…with everyone?"

Zoe nodded, but didn't get a chance to respond.

"I can grocery shop, but I can't cook worth a damn," Janet chimed in while waving a gallon of skim milk in the air. "Everybody else is too short on time. So we buy groceries, Zoe cooks three days a week, and every-body's happy."

Plus, she got to live on the cheap since everyone else paid for her food. Zoe didn't like her friends pointing out how poor she was, especially to Mr. International Super CEO, but it wasn't exactly a secret. So she smiled and turned to the oven to pull out three big meatloafs— one with extra barbecue sauce, one with extra egg and one made out of tofu. The salad was already on the table and Rachel, who worked at an ice-cream parlor, had brought home dessert.

In short, the meal was ready. If only she didn't die of embarrassment now. She loved her friends, but she could only imagine how casual—how cheap—her life must look to Stephen.

None of that showed in his expression, of course. He sat down, joined a moment of silent prayer, then politely answered every single one of the impertinent, probing and downright obnoxious questions that were thrown his way. It started with Rachel, who had rushed in with printed pages that she passed to anyone who would look.

"So…" Rachel began, "Zoe called you a mogul, and I thought she was exaggerating, but obviously not. You're practically a head of state! Look at this *Fortune* article. It names you as one of China's most favored sons."

Stephen didn't even glance at the print, but Zoe couldn't resist a peek. She'd just meant he acted like a Chinese mogul. She didn't really think he *was* one.

"Those articles are for publicity," he responded smoothly. "They do not accurately reflect reality."

"Well, Italian loafers come from somewhere," murmured Janet between bites of meatloaf. "Some of it's got to be true." She scanned the article. "What's a business incubator?"

That caught Zoe's attention. "Business incubator? I thought you were in pig farming."

Stephen nodded. "Pork is the core of my business."

Rachel passed over another seven sheets of paper. "But he's an incubator for like a dozen little businesses throughout China. Wigs, hats, even specialty foods—he does it all. One magazine called him 'the pork magnate who gives back.'"

Jesse frowned at her tomato juice and toyed with her slice of tofu-loaf. "Not all business incubators are good. Sure, the companies pretend to be a charity, helping start up new businesses—"

"What's an incubator?" Janet asked again, but Jesse was still talking.

"—but they can also exploit an ignorant population, abuse resources and run sweatshops." She pinned Stephen with a hard glare. "How much of a cut do you get out of each wig sale?"

"Nothing," Stephen answered. "We charge simple interest and—"

"What's an incubator!" Janet cried.

Everyone gasped at the girl's outburst, but it was Stephen who stepped in, smooth as silk. "My apologies. I get distracted when surrounded by such beauty." The line could have been corny, but he delivered it so quickly and so casually that no one had the chance to groan before he was moving on. "An incubator is a place where small businesses can grow. Think of it as a bank. We loan money, but we also offer advice, guidance, even basic accounting."

Janet smiled prettily. "Oh. Thanks for explaining."

"Yeah, okay," said Jesse, "but how does it all work—we need details."

"Of course," Stephen agreed. "My company tries to select by—" He took a bite of meatloaf and his eyes widened in surprise. "This is excellent food!"

Rachel chuckled. "Bet a guy like you never gets anything as plain as meatloaf."

"Certainly not one this delicious."

Zoe couldn't help herself. She warmed at the compliment. "Thank you—" she began, but was quickly lost amid an onslaught of questions.

Fortunately, Stephen continued to answer with wit and charm, mollifying even the suspicious Jesse. By the time the girls had to disappear to a class or study group, they had, one by one, given her a thumbs-up of approval. The last to leave was quiet Sarah, who had said absolutely nothing during the meal but had followed the conversation with bright, intelligent eyes. Sarah was a fellow graduate student, though in biochemistry not business, and the only one of her housemates who was the same age as Zoe.

"Don't clean up!" Sarah ordered firmly. "I haven't done anything at the house lately, and I feel really, really bad about it. So do me a favor and let me handle the dishes. I'll only be gone an hour." And with that she waved and disappeared.

Which left Zoe alone with Stephen. She leaned back in her chair, taking a deep breath before speaking from the heart. "I meant to apologize to you with a home-cooked meal, and instead you got subjected to an interrogation. Thank you for tolerating—"

"I did nothing I didn't choose to do, Zoe. They are

your friends and I was glad to meet them." His tone was firm, and she noticed a warmth in his eye. Could he really have meant it? He'd enjoyed it?

"Thank you," she whispered, touched to her core.

"And now I have a question for you," he said softly. "Did you study or meditate this afternoon?"

She frowned and shook her head. "Work, classes, then nap. That's it."

"No exercises?" He waved vaguely at the book he'd given her, which she'd set on the shelf that was her reserved space. "Something where you became quiet and…" He flushed slightly. "And thought about me?"

She bit her lip. Should she confess about holding the young Stephen in her sleep? Did she tell him—

He touched her arm. "Please. The truth is important."

She lifted her shoulder in an embarrassed shrug. "I thought about you. It's possible I fell asleep thinking about you. About holding you."

He nodded slowly, his pupils widening as he seemed to stare through her. "So it was real. It came from you."

"What? What was real?"

"Instead of booking my flight home, I fell asleep. That never happens. And I felt at peace for the first time in…" He shook his head. "I cannot remember how long."

She smiled. The awe in his voice was a beautiful thing. "I wish I could take credit for that, but—"

"I was held," he said firmly. "I was wrapped warm and secure in a woman's arms. I know it to be true, but no woman of my acquaintance would do such a thing. No one but you."

She stared at him. There were so many issues there. Dismissing the notion that he had somehow felt her innocent fantasy, she was stunned that he didn't have one woman in his life who would hold him. "Your mother—I'm sure…"

"No," he said. "She is long gone now, but even when she was alive, she was not a mothering kind of woman." His eyes grew distant. "She married my father for love, but it turned sour as love often does. So she contented herself with his money. I was an accident, I think."

"But that's awful!"

He shrugged, but she saw pain in his too-casual movement. "I had a home, servants and money. Many people would say I was extremely lucky."

"Not me," she said with a grunt. "But surely you know someone kind. You must have more women than just me. The tigresses—"

"Do you still not understand what I study?" he interrupted. "The practice is not about holding each other in comfort. It isn't even about love or tenderness. It's about raising your vibrational rate, about using the excitement of orgasm to step away from everything mundane in order to seek the divine. When you are lost to everything but sexual release, there is a small window to a higher plane. Everything stills and you can walk through to—"

"To love," she said, remembering the texts she'd read. "To joy."

He shook his head. "To purity. Peaceful stillness."

"Bull hockey," she returned, even though he jerked at her curt tone. "I've read the texts. They talk about love and joy."

He shook his head. "I have never experienced it as such. It has always been quiet. So beautifully peaceful." Then he leaned forward to touch her hand. "You are falling victim to an early error. Don't seek heaven thinking you will embrace an angel and fall passionately in love."

"I don't!"

"You do. Seek peace and stillness, instead. Though we use sex, the end is asexual. It is like pure crystal—clear and bright."

She bit her lip. "You're wrong," she said softly. "I may not be as experienced as you. I may have just started in this practice, but you're wrong. I feel it in my bones. You're struggling because you're not allowing heaven to be what heaven wants to be. You're limiting yourself, and therefore what you can experience."

She said the words, then abruptly flushed in mortification. Great, not only had she subjected him to an interrogation over dinner, now she'd once again challenged everything he thought or believed. He was about to say something biting, then leave. That's what Marty always did when she argued with him. Or worse, when she proved she knew more about something than he did. She believed Stephen was about to throw a male tantrum and braced herself for the blow. But he didn't. He simply looked at her, his brow narrowed in a fierce expression.

A few years ago, she would have apologized profusely and run away. She would have done anything to soothe his battered ego and forestall an argument. It was more important to her to stay in someone's good graces than to stand up for herself. But this was the new Zoe, post-divorce. She wasn't going to back down when she knew she was right.

And he didn't damn her for it. Instead, he simply arched a finely sculpted brow at her. "Prove it," he challenged.

She blinked. "What?"

"Partner with me again tonight. Climb to heaven and experience it for yourself."

She blinked. "I thought you intended to go back to

Hong Kong. That this was a waste of time and that we had different goals."

He nodded. "That was indeed what I thought. But you touched me this afternoon. You gave me sleep and peace. That is worth investigating, don't you think?" He flashed her a devastating grin. "I challenge you to prove that heaven has love and not just peace."

She gaped at him. "How? I could fake a meditative trance, come back and say anything I wanted."

He laughed. "You would not be able to lie convincingly."

"Maybe not, but that doesn't change the underlying fact that I'd be doing the experiencing and you'd be doing the watching."

"The only other option is for us to reverse last night. You would stimulate me, and I would make the climb."

She looked at him. Had he just maneuvered her into doing this for him? Well, it was only fair after last night. And the thought of going down on him was surprisingly exciting. Thrilling, even.

"You will be open to love? To joy? And not just try to manipulate the experience to what you think it ought to be?"

She expected him to laugh it off, to promise whatever she wanted so long as it got him off, but he didn't. He seemed to think long and deep. "I control things by my very nature. All men do, of course, but I like things very particular."

He didn't have to tell her that. Just looking at him, she knew that he was a precise man. A strong man with strong opinions. "Strength needs flexibility, too."

He nodded. "Very well. I am in America, and so I will try to think like an American."

She laughed. "What does that mean?"

"It means I will try to go with the flow." Then he abruptly leaned forward, stopping only when they were nose to nose. "Very well, Zoe, I accept your challenge. Do we try again tonight? Will you stroke and touch and tease me until I am begging for release? It will take a very, very long time."

This close to him, she could smell his exotic scent. Her mouth was dry and she licked her lips, stunned by how very much she wanted to do everything he asked and more. Then, when she saw his eyes focus on her mouth, she became even more daring. She darted her tongue out and pushed lightly between the seam of his lips. Then she pulled back.

"You're on, big boy. I'll show you how we do things American-style!"

7

"I'm beginning to feel a great fondness for hotel rooms," Zoe commented as they entered his suite.

Stephen shook his head. "The rooms I have reserved for practice in Hong Kong are ten times more luxurious than this."

"You have hotel rooms just for practice?"

He was shedding his coat and adjusting the thermostat again. "Hmm? No, no. Rooms in my home on Repulse Bay. Plus I always have access to the temple rooms, but I prefer my own home."

"Of course you would." The way he casually mentioned a temple in Hong Kong and a home on a bay made her anxious. She was a small-town girl, and now she was involved with a man who had separate rooms for sex practice. A man who lived in Hong Kong! It blew her mind even as it gave an unreal quality to this whole affair. Her mind flinched at the word *affair*, so she changed it to *partnership, challenge,* or maybe *evening exploit*. Then she had no more time to think because he was already preparing for whatever it was they were doing.

He started to light the candles, already half-burned from yesterday. Their scent tickled her nose, and she smiled. "Why don't you let me get those while you get ready?" She knew he wanted to meditate before they began.

He glanced up. "They need to be lit in a special order."

She nodded. "Clockwise around the room."

"With presence and intent."

She tilted her head. "Are you trying to control the experience?"

"Every part must be done correctly."

"Because I can't manage so difficult a task, right?" She held out her hand for the matches. He handed them over with a grimace.

"Most women appreciate it that I handle the mundane issues of the room."

"I think we've established that I'm not like your usual partners."

He had no answer for that except a warm smile. She moved about the room lighting candles and visualizing the light burning away all her excess thoughts and stray emotional clutter. The room was filled with stillness. Peace. Quiet. And Stephen was stark-naked.

She swallowed, trying not to watch how his skin glowed golden in the candlelight. He was lying completely flat, disdaining the use of a pillow. He'd stripped the blankets and top sheet off the bed, so it was just him stretched out on white cotton. Except for the glossy black strands of hair on the pillowcase, his body was completely hairless. Completely.

She smiled, liking the sight of his penis lying thick and heavy against his thigh. It wasn't jutting hard yet, but it would be. And she got to hold it, stroke it and do whatever she wanted with it. With all of him, actually. Her mouth watered at the idea.

"I will try to remain in a meditative state throughout the whole process. Do not be surprised if I lie as if dead."

She repressed a snort of laughter. "Is that a challenge, Mr. Chu?"

He cracked an eye at her. "I have done this for many years, Zoe."

"*This* meaning lying completely still while a woman tends to you?"

He nodded. "I will be meditating, taking the stimulation you provide and using it to excite my internal cauldron."

"And in this way you hope to experience heaven. A peaceful, still kind of heaven."

He smiled benevolently at her. "Exactly so."

"Wrong," she shot back. "Don't forget our deal. You are going to be open to whatever experience comes. Whatever heaven or hell or emotion floods your body, you need to allow it. Ride that tigress—"

"Dragon," he corrected. "I am a man. I ride a dragon."

"Ride the beast, whatever it is, but allow the experience to just *be* without trying to direct it. Agreed?"

"Agreed." He took a full deep breath, and Zoe couldn't help but admire how his chest expanded with the motion, broadening, lengthening and then releasing. Then he closed his eyes and—yes—lay as if he were dead. His hands were folded across his chest and his face was completely composed. He could indeed have been lying in his own coffin. Except for the being-naked part.

Zoe approached the bed, looking down at him as she considered her plan of attack, so to speak. She could just grab hold and start up, but that was rather crude and certainly wasn't her style. She'd been grabbed and fondled too fast and too hard before. It wasn't pleasant. She needed a more subtle approach. But what?

She settled down on the bed near his right shoulder. Close enough to touch, and able to see his entire body. "The first time I saw a man's penis I was in second grade."

He cracked an eye. "How old is second grade?"

She did a swift calculation. "Eight years old. There was a *Playgirl* magazine that had been discarded in the park where I used to play. My best friend dared me to turn the pages."

"It is customary to allow the partner to meditate in silence," he said. There was no trace of annoyance in his statement. Just a simple correction of her form or whatever. So she stretched out her hand and flicked the tip of his penis with her fingernail.

"Ouch!" He sat bolt upright and glared at her. "That is not a bully club, Zoe! My organ is—"

"Going to be flicked like that if you try to control this situation again." He stared at her, and she arched her brows in response. Finally, he huffed backward onto the bed.

"That hurt!" he groused.

Impulsively, she leaned down and gave his penis a quick kiss. "Sorry you made me cause you pain," she said. She lingered there a moment, looking closer. Then she inhaled. As a rule, she hadn't thought men's scent all that appealing. But perhaps it was just a reflection of the men she'd been with. Stephen's scent was completely different than she'd expected: clean and musky, if that were possible. There was a hint of spice, but that perhaps came from the candles. Mostly, she smelled him, strong and potent. And completely intriguing.

"The kisses do not hurt," he said.

She flicked his penis again, but lightly.

He still gasped. "I wasn't trying to direct," he said. "I was merely making a comment."

"I ought to tie you up."

He gestured with one hand. "There are bindings in the suitcase."

"Is there a gag, too?"

He opened his eyes. "At this rate, I will reach heaven when I die and not before."

She smiled, unaccountably pleased to see a flash of humor in him. "When one meditates," she said, mimicking his lofty tone, "it is customary to be silent."

"There is an English phrase that fits…" He frowned for a moment. "Oh, yes. Yadda, yadda." He even made the hand motion of a mouth flapping.

She cracked up. She couldn't help it. "And here I thought you had no sense of humor at all."

His gaze canted away, but not before she saw a sudden vulnerability there. "You are not the first to say that," he said softly. "I do, though. Truly, I do."

"I know you do," she said. Then she leaned back a bit to look at him. "You're stretched out naked, waiting for me to do gosh-only-knows-what to your body. And the first sign of vulnerability is when I make a joke about your sense of humor?"

He swallowed, a lightning bolt of a sign that he was feeling embarrassed. "I have no fear that you will hurt my body."

Only his spirit, she realized. He feared she didn't like him, his sense of humor and…what else? she wondered. "I know so little about you," she murmured.

"Partners do not need to know about each other to practice. In many ways, anonymity is easier."

"But not better," she said. "Definitely not better."

He shrugged. "That remains to be seen."

She thought about that for a moment. "I'll bet you've gone the anonymous sex route a zillion times."

He nodded, but did not comment.

"Have you ever known your partner personally? Every detail about them?"

"You can never know every detail about someone," he said softly. She opened her mouth to comment—or flick his penis—but he forestalled her by lifting his fingers. "Everyone attaches to their first partner. It is inevitable."

"And?" she pressed.

"And she was a poor girl from mainland China with little education and a love of shiny things. She hid her lust for money well, but these things come out over time. She liked having a rich partner. She liked it when I gifted her with silks and began hinting about jewelry."

Zoe grimaced. "What kind of jewelry? Pretty-necklace kind of jewelry? Or the wedding-ring kind?"

"Both. First I ignored it, thinking I must have misunderstood. She was a serious tigress, and tigresses do not marry."

That's not what Zoe had heard from Tracy, but she didn't say that. Instead, she put her hand on Stephen's thigh and idly traced the contour of the muscles there. "And did she get more insistent?"

"She did. When I couldn't explain it away again, I simply ended the partnership."

There was a flatness in his tone that told her he was covering pain. "She wasn't the only one, was she?"

"I did not get as close to my other partners."

"But they all wanted your money in the end." It wasn't a question.

He looked directly at her, and the openness she saw

in his eyes surprised her. She expected that he would have cut himself off emotionally from this discussion. Instead, she saw a silent longing. Then he blinked and it was gone.

"It is human nature to want pretty things. Who wouldn't like silk sheets or servants to cook and serve delicacies every night?"

"I can't imagine," she said, and she meant it. She couldn't imagine a life like that. It was so beyond her experience that it sounded more like a fairy tale. "Did you try giving up the luxuries? Practicing at the temple?"

He nodded. "It didn't matter. They all knew who I was. And often it was more convenient for me to just have the girl brought in and fed beforehand. Besides, I *like* giving gifts if it works out. If the experience is good."

She winced. "Rewards for a job well done. You make them sound like hookers." Then before he could comment, she squeezed his thigh. "I know. It's a serious practice. Heaven. Enlightenment. Yadda, yadda. But I just can't shake the feeling that what your practice lacks is an emotional connection to another."

"One cannot attain heaven while still being tied to Earth."

And there it was, the crux of her issues with tigress tantrism: it was all so cold. Stimulation, meditation, enlightenment. Sure it felt good at first, but in the end, it sounded empty to her. Not the way Nathan and Tracy talked about it, of course. But for Stephen? Practice for him sounded more like a bank transaction.

Until now, she decided. She was going to make it different. She was going to make it personal. Unfortunately, she couldn't force him to open up to her.

Somehow she doubted he would start sharing childhood memories while she was stroking his penis. So that meant she would be the one talking.

"I'm going to start your practice now," she said softly. "I'll probably ask you questions. Don't feel like you have to respond. Not unless you want to."

"Are you going to hurt me if you don't like my answer?"

She grinned. "Only if your answer comes in the form of an order."

"Fair enough," he agreed. Then he closed his eyes, once again taking that deep breath that expanded his beautiful chest.

"My, you're pretty," she said. She reached up to stroke the ridge of his collarbone. "Oh, yeah, that's what I was going to tell you. I gotta say, a man's penis really isn't all that good-looking. That's what I thought when I was eight and things haven't changed much. It's still this thick thing that dangles and gets in the way. That's what I kept thinking. It must just get in the way when you're running around, climbing, putting on pants."

She glanced down at him. His penis was thicker now, but not completely full yet. And damn if the sight didn't still look weird to her, and yet deep down she felt an ache. It might not be pretty, but oh, she wanted to feel it inside her.

"Anyway," she continued, "I have a thing for men's chests. Broad shoulders, deep collarbone, and those sweet flat nipples." Her hand followed her words, stroking across his smooth skin, knowing the muscle was just beneath, and then ending up at his nipple. It had already tightened to a small knot, and she brushed her thumb across it.

"I read that some men's nipples are more sensitive than a woman's. Is that true?" She glanced at his face. His eyes were closed, and his nostrils flared with his breathing. She watched the steady rise and fall of his chest, wondering if his breath was more rapid than before. His erection was certainly pushing harder toward her.

Then she shrugged. "I don't know if it's true. I just know that I like the feel of men's nipples." And so saying, she leaned down and ran the flat of her tongue across his left one. It was like rolling across a metal stud, only he was hot, not cool. She toyed with the little nub, letting it push against her tongue, then flicking it back. Eventually, she added teeth and suction in little nips. Truthfully, she was doing just what she liked done to her. She simply enjoyed the sensations against her mouth, and so she allowed herself to play.

She also enjoyed the sound of his breath coming in a harder tempo. He liked this. Good, she thought with a smile. She did, too. So she switched to the other nipple and did the same there.

But then she grew bored. His penis was at full alert, and she was feeling a little hot and bothered herself. Plus, he'd turned the thermostat up to toasty, so she felt perfectly justified in pulling off her shirt. She had a red cami on underneath. And frankly, her jeans were feeling really restrictive, so she took those off as well, leaving her matching panties on underneath. Too bad his eyes were closed, so he couldn't appreciate the look.

She spent a little more time stroking and teasing his upper body, but it was merely a prelude. It was time for the main course, and so she slowly kissed her way down his body.

"Sex for me has always been too hurried, you know?"

she said as she allowed her hair to brush across his belly. His flat abdomen rippled at that, and so she spent some time on his belly trying to make it happen again. She succeeded twice. "It's not like I have a lot of time. And when I was married, it was never about me. Marty wanted to get to the main event, and so there was never much exploration."

Thoughts of her ex were souring her mood, so she pushed them aside and trailed her tongue down from his navel. Stephen obviously shaved because the skin was as smooth as the rest of his body, and she found she liked it. She took her time touching the velvety skin around his groin. It was stretched tight and hard, but it still felt vellum-soft against her fingers. His balls were pulled up taut, and she spent a great deal of time stroking and touching the skin there. She'd never examined a man's sac before, and she found it an interesting part of his body. Especially interesting was the way Stephen's breath shortened as she held him, moving and tugging on him just the tiniest bit.

The whole process made her incredibly hot, and she couldn't stop herself from arching her body up along his. But her cami was in the way, and her panties were wet. And he was harder than a rock and so perfectly poised for her.

So she stripped off the last of her clothes. She wanted to be skin to skin with him. This time when she rubbed herself against him, she was the one who gasped. Her breasts were swollen, her nipples hard, and each time she moved over him, hot bolts of fire shot through her chest. Her abdomen felt as tight as his looked and her womb felt liquid. How long had it been since she'd had a man inside her? Too long. Much too long.

But this wasn't about her. It was about his meditations to heaven, so she crawled back down his body. She licked his penis. She stroked it with hand and tongue and teeth. She even used suction and a variety of tigress techniques she had read from the texts.

His head was arched back, and his Adam's apple bounced as he swallowed. His breath was coming hard, but even so he seemed completely controlled. Every one of his tigress partners would have done what she was doing. As far as he was concerned, this was the same ol', same ol'.

She sighed. Despite her bold claims, there was nothing she could do for him that dozens of more experienced women hadn't already done. And that made her sad. She had wanted to be special for him. Sure her pride was involved, but more than that, he seemed liked a man searching for something. She had hoped, for a little bit at least, to be what he wanted.

"I have a confession to make," she said as she once again rolled her body up his. Lord, she would never get tired of doing that. Especially when she rubbed her nipples over every single ripple of abs and ribs and collarbone. She did it again, just because it felt so good.

"I lied about fantasizing about you earlier." She settled her cleft over his erection. He was thrusting upward, but she came from below, sliding her folds up and down his penis. She was fairly flexible this way, her hips moving in long slow strokes that made her moan in hunger.

"Where was I?" she murmured after a while. "Oh, yeah, confessions. I was thinking about you, but not the adult you. Well, yeah, there were adult fantasies, too, but this afternoon I was thinking about the kid you."

She was getting too hot this way, so she crawled forward over him. Then she kept crawling until her nipple dangled just over his mouth. Without even thinking about what she was doing, she rolled the hardened point across the seam of his lips. First one breast then the other. Back and forth.

To her surprise, he opened his mouth and sucked it in. The shock had her gasping as his tongue gave those wonderful flicks.

She was going to come just from his tongue, and that would be completely embarrassing. Orgasming all over him when she was supposed to be the one taking him to heaven? Nothing doing. So she reluctantly pulled back. But he didn't seem to want to let her go. He tugged on her nipple until her arms began to shake. Then she pushed away hard, and her breast came out of his mouth with a pop.

"You keep making me forget what I'm talking about. What I'm trying to say here is that I don't know much about you, but I can guess. From things you've said, I guessed that you had a pretty sad childhood. Poor little rich boy is such a cliché, but I think you lived it. And I'm so sad for you."

She leaned down to kiss his forehead, then his eyes, then his cheeks.

"And that got me to thinking," she said. "Not in words so much as feelings and memories. I had all these dreams when I got married. It would be a hard road, but Marty and I were going to get our degrees then have children. White picket fence and all."

She leaned down farther to rub her lips across his. She couldn't feel his breath, not really. It almost seemed like he held it back. His chin was still lifted so she had a good angle on his mouth and she spoke straight into his slightly parted lips.

"I don't want to be your mother or anything. That's just…well, twisted. But I want to be a mother, and no one should grow up lonely. So I pretended I held you as a boy. I gave you the love you should have had a long time ago."

She swallowed, lifting herself up to look down into his face. His eyes were open, she realized with shock, and she leaned down to kiss them closed. She didn't like him looking at her when she was speaking so openly.

"So there you have my deep dark secret," she said as she pulled back. "I want to have kids. I'm just finishing up my degree, will get a job and work my ass off for another decade at least, and I'm not giving any of that up for a man or his family. I'm not. But deep down, a part of me really wishes to throw it all away on kids. Dark-haired, dark-eyed, half-Chinese kids whose father is a rich Chinese aristocrat with a beautiful, beautiful body."

She smiled and nipped his nose. "There. That was my fantasy." Then she sighed. "So you know, I'm on the pill. And I know you've got a clean bill of health, so this isn't about trapping you or anything. I just want to pretend— for a little bit—that I can have my fantasy. I can be a mother and have my career and my Chinese mogul in one perfect moment of bliss."

So saying, she adjusted her hips and pushed down on him. He slipped inside with such ease, and yet she felt stretched and filled in every part. When she looked at him this time, she didn't mind that his eyes were open. He was looking at her with such surprise, such stunned shock that she almost laughed.

Instead, she gave him her warmest smile. "I know this is supposed to be about you, but I know I can't compare to your other women. You win the contest, Stephen. I couldn't give you a perfect moment of bliss."

She licked her lips. "So please forgive me for stealing this moment for me."

She took a deep breath, arching her back as she slowly slid up his penis then back down. One long stroke, but she felt it in every part of her.

His hands moved. They had been at his sides, but now they slid up her legs to grip her hips. His hands tightened on her there, and she knew he had agreed.

She smiled. "Thank you," she whispered. "Thank you, Stephen."

Then she bore down with her pelvis and let him thrust.

8

STEPHEN'S CONCENTRATION shattered. He had been straining for a while, holding on to his meditation by the barest thread. But not anymore. Now everything splintered into a thousand shards, leaving him naked and vulnerable before her.

How had this happened? There were tigresses who liked to chatter, but few ever tried during practice. Even the most talkative settled at those moments into quiet absorption, meditation and the ebb and flow of energy. But not Zoe.

When she'd first begun to talk, he'd meant to reprimand her. He *had* reprimanded her. It made no difference. She was intent on trying her own babbling path, and so he decided to ignore her. He was advanced enough to meditate through any distraction, or so he believed.

But five minutes into her whatever-it-was—monologue—he realized that what she was saying was important. It came first as an awareness of her energy. Her breath shimmered power across his skin that flowed into his body. It took him a moment to realize that it came from her words or through her words. He didn't know, but when he looked—really looked—he could see that she was pouring her yin into him. Through her words.

Then he began to listen. And listening, he became enraptured with what she said even more than what she did. His usual technique was to tune out his partner completely. His focus was on his own experience as he channeled the energy into his core. But with Zoe, his inner circle expanded to include her. She and her words became a central part of his energy field. And she was wonderful!

She appeared to his inner eyes as an incandescent light, glowing warm and bright. But as she talked, she opened up a stream from her center and allowed it to drop onto him. Slowly at first, but then larger, wider and ever more beautiful. He spent long moments just looking at her, barely understanding what she was saying but completely absorbed in seeing her pour herself into him.

Then she said she wanted children. That she wanted *his* children. He heard the sadness in her voice, understood the choices she was making. He even agreed with her decision, but at that moment, he could see the ache in her heart for a child that could never be. *His* child that would never be born. And his concentration shattered.

It happened before she surrounded him. Before he thrust into her like a man driven by lust. But any hope of regaining his focus disappeared the moment she slipped her tight, wet sheath around him. His meditation was lost, and the experience became wholly and completely about her. He could still see her light in his inner eye. He could see the way her energies churned and swirled as he thrust into her. And it was so beautiful that he did it again and again.

He held her hips pinned steady, gripping them as he would a lifeline. And he pistoned into her, allowing his yang power to merge with her yin. He put all of his focus into her just as she had done for him. And between them both, the energy grew hotter and brighter.

Dragon men did not release their seed. Dragon men did not give their regenerative power away. And of all dragon men, he was the most virile alive today. His yang essence had been cleansed by the strictest regimen, his energy was absolutely pure, and he never, ever wasted even a drop of it.

But he would for her. He knew it before he saw her skin flush rosy from her exertions. Her breasts were pointed and bouncing as she moved, and the arch of her throat stretched beautifully long. Her body was sweet and soft, curving in at her waist and flaring into perfect hips and toned legs. Her orgasm began with a sudden arch that had her breath suspended on a cry of ecstasy, and the view of her physical body was lovely. But in spirit, she was astounding, this woman who mourned because she could not have his child.

He thrust into her with a grunt of effort, holding off his orgasm to prolong hers. It was hard because she had brought him to his most primal self, the animal in him that pounded inside a woman, that took what he wanted and claimed it for his own. That primal man was infinitely powerful as he branded this woman with every penetration. Zoe was his. And she would make their child.

That was what his primal self believed, and Stephen gloried in it. So when the rush overwhelmed him, he did not fight it. His yang compressed and tightened, then shot from him into her, and he roared in triumph at what he had done. He gave it all to her, to this woman who wanted his child.

She was his!

The energy exploded out of him and mixed with hers. They could have made a child. Or they would have if modern medicine hadn't prevented it. Of that he was certain. If things were different. If their choices were different.

So rather than a child, the two of them were remade instead. The creative energy surrounded them in a bubble of power. It swirled through them both, mixed and merged, forming and reforming all that they were. He ought to be afraid, but in that bubble of power, there was no fear. There was only the amazing power of...

Love. A mother's love for her child. A babe's trust and adoration of his parents. In that moment, he was both child and parent, generations upon generations throughout time, linked through love—sometimes twisted, sometimes ugly, but always there in some form. Love, pure and beautiful for all its variations.

He felt the love, was the love, and looking at Zoe, he saw that she was an integral part of the unbroken chain. Mother, mate and daughter, just as he was father, mate and son—all in one.

And he was healed.

HE WOKE SLOWLY, his mind lingering in wonder, his body heavy with discomfort. It was a distant ache, a quiet voice easily ignored for the moment. Or maybe not so easy because it pulled him away from the glorious love and deeper into his body.

He breathed. On some level, he knew he was returning from the heavenly realm. His body would feel—did feel—heavy and cold while his spirit wished to linger in that bright beautiful place that was...that had been...that still whispered through his core.

Love. Creative, generational and ever-present love from parent to child to grandchild and beyond. He felt it, he knew it, and it remained even as his awareness returned to his body.

He was lying naked on the bed, but he wasn't cold. A warm body—Zoe—curled against his side, her tiny hand resting lightly on his chest. A sheet covered them both, but he hardly needed it. She was all the warmth he would ever require.

He turned his head toward her and dropped a kiss on her blond hair. A first for him, he realized after he'd done it. He did not kiss his partners after practice was done. Certainly not when they were asleep, and definitely not so tenderly. But he kissed Zoe, and then he wrapped his arm around her and tried to draw her tighter to his side.

She woke with a gasp. "You're awake!" She blinked twice and pushed the hair out of her eyes. "Are you all right? Do you need water or anything? When you went into your trance, I didn't know what to do. So I called Nathan. He said to let you rest. That when you woke, you'd have to go slow. You're returning to your body."

I know, he said. Or thought he did. He heard no sound. Then with an effort of will, he forced his mouth to form words. "You're amazing."

She stared at him for a moment, then dimpled prettily. "Well, okay, so maybe Nathan was wrong. He said you'd come out of the trance angry. He warned me that you might be very vicious."

Yes, Stephen thought, many did come away from heaven angry because they had to leave. But he still felt the love inside him. Deep down, underneath his thoughts and his body, he felt a core of steady love. "This must be how it feels to have good parents."

Zoe frowned. "Uh…right. You're not making much sense now, but that's okay. Take your time."

He grinned. "When you have good parents, you feel love even as an adult. No matter what, you know they love you. Even when they are gone, you know, deep down, that you are loved."

She nodded. "Yes."

"I feel it now. As if it had been. As if it always was." He took a deep breath, trying to order his thoughts. They refused to coalesce. "I can't explain it, but I feel it. I feel like my parents loved me."

She didn't comment. It was clear she didn't know what to say, but he didn't care. He could still see the aura around her, the glow of wonder that was all Zoe. Sweet heaven, she was beautiful.

"Thank you," he said. The words didn't come close to expressing the oceans of gratitude he felt at that moment, but they were all he had. "Thank you so very, very much."

She flushed a bright pink. "Believe me when I say it was my pleasure." Then she bit her lip, searching his face. "Nathan said something about a special tea. I should make you—"

He tightened his grip on her side. "Don't move. Wait with me. Just…stay here."

She nodded, then relaxed against his side. He found he wanted to hear her talk again. It didn't matter what, he just wanted to hear her voice. "Tell me what happened," he said. "Tell me what you experienced."

"Shouldn't that be my line? I mean, you're the one who went to heaven." Then she frowned. "You did go, didn't you?"

"Yes," he said, then shook his head. "But I can't make sense of it yet. Tell me what you remember."

"Besides one of the greatest orgasms of my life? Oh, my, it went on and on. I felt cold and hot and ecstatic all at once. And then it was…perfect. Just perfect in a single moment of…perfection." She shrugged, and he liked the feel of her skin brushing along his. "I guess I'm not making much sense."

"I understand you. Did you feel the love, Zoe? I thought you were there with me. Did you feel—"

"Yes," she rushed to say. "I felt it. I felt you. And it was…" She took a deep breath.

"Perfect," he finished for her.

She nodded, and they shared a moment of complete accord. But eventually, her eyes grew troubled. "I came out of it earlier than you did. You were just lying there, your eyes glazed, but so very, very bright."

"A trance. I'm sorry, did it frighten you?"

"A little. But I've read the texts, so I wasn't completely thrown. That's when I found your phone and called Nathan. And he said—"

"Make teas, keep me warm and that I'd come out of it angry."

She nodded. "Are you sure you don't want to curse or something? I'll understand."

He laughed. The sound was rough and unsteady, but it felt so wonderful. Had he ever truly laughed before? "I don't want to curse, Zoe. I feel…" Loved. "I feel…" Happy. A happiness he'd never felt before. "I feel…like I need a bathroom."

She raised her eyebrows, and he must have done the same. He hadn't even realized what the discomfort was that brought him back to his body. But now that he named it, the need rapidly became urgent. He reluctantly released her and rolled to his side.

"Take it slow. I've got you." And she did. She helped him shift to his side then put weight on his feet. It was ridiculous that he could feel so wonderful and yet find his own feet difficult to control. But if it meant he kept her at his side, so much the better. She scrambled out of bed and supported him as he hobbled to the bathroom. Fortunately, by the time they made it there, he had discovered coordination and the ability to stand on his own.

"I've got it now," he said. "Thanks."

She nodded and stepped outside while he took care of business. Meanwhile, she started to chatter on the other side of the door.

"Nathan said I should watch you. There were things that could go wrong. And I did…for a time." He could hear the regret in her voice. "After about a half hour, your breathing deepened. Your eyes fluttered shut, and you looked like you were sleeping."

When he came out of the bathroom, she was leaning against the wall, her jeans and cami already pulled on.

"I fell asleep, Stephen. I'm sorry. I was so tired, and you looked like you were sleeping—"

He pressed a finger to her lips. "You ascended as well. Maybe not as long as I did, but you were still recovering. If we were at the temple, you would have had two tigresses watching over your rest. As it was, you had to care for me."

She grimaced. "But I didn't care for you. I fell asleep."

He let his hand slide from her mouth to her neck, then behind it to draw her into a kiss. He used no skill as he pressed his mouth to hers. None of his dragon techniques came to mind. He simply wanted to touch her again, deeply and intimately. So he kissed her, and he kept kissing her until she softened against him.

It was a long time until they separated. They were both breathing hard, but by mutual consent, neither went beyond the long kiss. It was too soon for more. He still needed hours of meditation to process what had happened. And yet, as he gazed into her wide blue eyes, he already knew what had occurred.

She had healed him. He was healed of the lingering chill of a cold and distant childhood. Sure, he'd made peace with his past a long time ago. But the chill had remained, the quiet center that once said he was unlovable. That cold center was gone. And the joy of that was beyond imagining.

"I will order breakfast," he said. "Whatever you like. Then we can talk and plan for our next…" His voice trailed away as she shook her head.

"I have to go to class," she said. Then she gestured to the window and the daylight that poured through the sheers.

He looked at the clock and saw that it was nearly nine in the morning. Lord, he had promised Jiao Kai he would make certain decisions by eight. But after last night, all of that seemed so unimportant.

"I really have to go, Stephen. I don't want to, but I need to get my MBA. It's what I've been working toward for years."

He nodded, trying to order his thoughts. "When can I see you again? We need to set up a schedule, a plan for continuing."

"I don't know," she said, sounding truly distressed. "I have a paper due tomorrow and I have to work. This whole thing started as just a fun distraction, way back when. But now…" She bit her lip, and her eyes went soft. "It's so much more, Stephen, but I've got a group project due. And I'm struggling in class."

"Forget all that. This is more important." He had

meant the words for himself more than her. As she had been detailing her classwork, he had been thinking of meetings that shouldn't be delayed, reports to filter through and the endless pile of paperwork. So it was a bit of a shock when she answered with a slow and deliberate coldness.

"No, Stephen, I won't."

He blinked, bringing his attention firmly and wholly back to her. "What?"

"Don't get me wrong, I want to keep pursuing this. I do. It was…"

"Perfect," he said. "Yes, it was. Please, we have to keep going."

She grimaced, her sigh coming from her entire body. "I want to, Stephen, but I have plans. I won't give up my degree this close to finishing. I have to focus on school for a few days. Just a couple of days, I swear."

Days? He had to be back in Hong Kong in a few days. "Let's not make any decisions right now. It's too fast, and—"

"And I have to get to class."

"Yes." He nodded. "You have class. I have business." He gestured to his laptop. "Give me your cell number. I'll call you. When is your class over?"

"I don't have a cell phone."

He stared. Who didn't have a phone?

"I have e-mail. The university gives me one. But I have to go to work after class."

He shook his head. "Quit your job. I'll pay your rent. I'll take care of all that for you." It was the wrong thing to say. He watched her back stiffen, and her eyes grow impossibly cold.

"I don't think so," she said quietly.

"Do you not understand how precious this is? I have searched my whole life for you. For what happened here last night." He touched her arms lightly, but she held herself so stiffly that he didn't dare increase the contact. "Zoe, we have to keep going!"

"I won't be your mistress."

He frowned. "What? What are you talking about?"

She bit her lip, closing her eyes as she visibly pulled herself together. He watched it happen with a growing sense of panic, and when she opened them again, she felt closed off to him. He tried to feel her energy with his inner eye, but all he got was a dark wall of nothing.

"What's wrong, Zoe? Why are you moving away like this?"

"You're making me think about it, Stephen. About throwing it all away just for a man. For you. But I won't do that! I won't give up my degree." She walked toward the door, but he grabbed her arms and turned her toward him.

"There's something else. There's something deeper. What happened that you haven't told me about? Why are you suddenly afraid?"

"I'm not. I'm just confused. And disoriented. And I have to go to class!"

She was getting more upset by the second. He didn't want to let her go, was afraid that if she left him now, he would never breach the wall between them. But he could tell that pushing now would only make things worse. He didn't want to step away. Every part of him wanted to tie her down to the bed until they worked out exactly what was going on. But he knew that would only make things worse.

So he clamped down his Neanderthal feelings and stepped back. "At least give me your e-mail. Please."

She hesitated a moment, then quickly wrote it down on the hotel pad. "And here's the phone number of my house. You can always leave a message there."

He nodded, pleased to see that bit of softening in her. She had given him a way to contact her. But he wanted so much more!

"Zoe—" he began.

"I have to go." She grabbed her coat and dashed out of the room.

9

ZOE FOUND IT HARD to focus in class. The niceties of financial modeling just did not hold her attention. Not after last night.

Stephen was right. She had experienced much more than simple heaven. Ecstatic orgasm? Yes. A body that still tingled with little happy flashes in not-so-appropriate places? Oh, yes! But what shook her to the core was the love. Total and overwhelming love that made her feel whole and so filled with joy that she could barely contain it.

It kept her horribly distracted in class, and it was worse later when she was supposed to be counting bagels at work. People kept catching her staring into space and smiling. It wasn't a full-out grin or goofy-kid happiness. This was an inner glow that she found hard to suppress. It started deep inside and filtered out by way of a soft, secret curve to her lips. Then she would get lost in memory and just stare at nothing as her body heated and her back stretched.

That was the weirdest part. In those moments, she felt just like a cat slowly waking from a long sleep. Her back would stretch, her eyes slip shut and she would want to dig her claws in something as she lengthened her spine into a feline stretch. It was as if she really were a tigress, just waking up. Except she wasn't waking, she was staring off into space and *not* counting bagels. And besides, she was a dog person, not a cat person. But wow, there were times when she even felt as though she had a cat's tail and would whip it around playfully as she walked or, worse, stretched to grab something from the top rack.

"Oooh, baby," her coworker cooed from behind the sandwich register. "You got something fine in you last night."

She turned to stare at Anne, a redheaded high-school basketball player who was as white as whipped cream, but somehow made her voice sound ghetto. "What are you talking about?" Zoe shot back in her best I-outrank-you voice.

Anne raised her hands in defense, slipping back into her normal flat Midwestern accent. "Hey, I'm just saying you look good today."

Zoe arched her brow. "I'm in uniform with a ponytail. I look as good as I always do."

Anne shook her head. "Nope. Something different. Something good. And maybe it has something to do with that fine bit of hunka-hunka sitting over there." She gestured at the table right in front of the fire where Stephen sat.

He was dressed casually for him: dark jeans—designer—and an emerald-green sweater. His hair fell artfully forward across his brow, and he sipped his espresso with every appearance of rapture. And then he looked at her, and Zoe's breath caught in her throat. She saw hunger there, a burning need that made the tigress in her simultaneously flex her claws and purr in delight. Against her will, her spine stretched, shoulders rolled back and down, and her lips felt dry. So she licked them and watched his eyes zero in on the motion. Then she flushed in embarrassment and turned away, biting her lower lip in mortification. Unfortunately, she had turned toward Anne, who was smirking as only a teenage girl can.

"What?" Zoe snapped. "It's not what you think!" Of course, it was *exactly* what Anne thought, but Zoe was too flustered right then to form a coherent thought.

Anne's grin just widened as she pulled the inventory sheet out of Zoe's lax fingers. "Go on. I got you covered."

Zoe resolutely pulled a bagel bin out and dropped it on the counter. "I'm busy. I don't need to be—"

"He said he just wants to talk to you. Five minutes."

Zoe tightened her back muscles, fighting the need to rush to Stephen's side for whatever reason. "I'm working! I can't drop everything just because he showed up. I'm a manager here! I have responsibilities."

Anne laughed. "You're counting bagels, not doing brain surgery. And you haven't taken your break yet." The girl physically turned her around and pushed her toward the main seating area.

"I can't—"

"Did you notice he ordered you a coffee?" Anne added in her ear. "Caramel latte extra whip."

Zoe shot a glare at her friend. "You told!"

"He asked what your most favorite sin-food was. So yeah, I told. He gave me a twenty-dollar tip!"

Zoe groaned. "He doesn't even know what that's worth. He's used to Chinese currency."

Anne didn't even blush. "So make it worth his while." Then she shoved Zoe out from behind the counter. It didn't take much effort. Zoe'd known it was a losing battle halfway through her first morning class.

Last night had been too amazing for her to resist Stephen for long. And halfway across the floor to his table, she couldn't quite remember what her problem with him was anyway.

He looked up as she slid in across from him. His eyes held the same intensity she'd felt across the room, but up close, there was an almost electric quality to the air. She started tingling again, deep in her belly, and her nipples tightened. She was thankful she'd worn a padded bra, so he wasn't likely to notice, but she did, and it feel both great and awful at the same time. Great because—well, sex was fun. Awful because she could not afford the time or energy to indulge in fun sex, even if it made her mouth water—and not for her latte.

"Hi, Stephen," she managed. "What brings you here?"

"You, of course," he returned. "I need to talk to you."

"We can't get together tonight, Stephen. I just can't. I haven't the time." She said the words all in a rush, trying to get them out before she changed her mind. "I want to. You can't know how much I want to, but it's all been so fast. And I've been working so long to get my degree. You make me forget all of that, and I just can't. I need to graduate. With a degree, I can get a good job. And with a good job, I won't ever have to worry about all my money disappearing with a stolen Visa. I won't have to rely on my parents for rent. I'll be secure. Please say you understand."

"I do." He dipped his chin in quiet acceptance and she didn't know whether to feel hurt or happy at that. Then she waited in tense silence as she watched him toy with his espresso cup. Was he nervous? Was he as confused about last night as she was? They had done so much, it had been so incredible that she was still processing it all. Was he as thrown as she was? He didn't seem to be, but then again, she barely knew him, right? It wasn't like they had gone through the usual dating rituals before hopping into bed.

"Um, Stephen…" she began, but then her voice faltered. She didn't know what she wanted to say, so she ended up ducking her head into her latte and slurping it noisily like a four-year-old. She grimaced at the sound, then set her cup down. "Sorry. I actually do know how to eat in polite company."

He frowned. "What?"

She gestured at her latte. "Slurping. I know that's not polite."

"What? Oh. That sometimes happens with hot liquids and whipped cream."

"Um. Yeah. But I bet most of your women don't slurp even through mile-high foam."

He tilted his head, his brows narrowed in confusion. "I don't know. The women I know drink tea."

Of course they did. After all, he lived in freaking China. She sighed. "See, that's the problem, Stephen. We are just so different."

His lips thinned. "So there is a problem. This morning you would not admit that much."

She rubbed a palm across her right eye, pushing harder against the bony ridge to ease the headache building there. "I'm tired. Last night was great. I couldn't concentrate in class. And now, my head hurts, I still have to write that paper for tomorrow, and since I have to pick up extra shifts, it'll be Sunday noon before I catch a break. Don't ask me about problems, Stephen. I can't tell where one ends and the next begins."

"You're tired, overwhelmed by everything we've been doing, and your ex stole your rent money."

She nodded. That pretty much summed it up.

"I've paid your rent for the rest of the school year."

She blinked, her entire body growing still and cold. It was like a magic get-out-of-jail-free card, and the relief that rolled through her was as seductive as it was terrifying.

"I can't accept that," she finally said. "I want to and it's very nice of you. But no."

"It's a loan, Zoe. And it comes with a price."

She set down her coffee, and took a deep breath. "Well, at least you're honest. Blunt but honest."

He didn't comment. She felt his eyes on her, calm and steady, but when she looked deeper she found she couldn't read him at all. His emotions were hidden behind that blank expression. She was so busy studying his face that she didn't at first notice when he pushed a paper toward her. Then it hit her hand, and she stared down in shock.

"That looks like a plane ticket," she said softly.

"Voucher. No date. Come out to Hong Kong for a week. Devote yourself fully to our practice for a week."

She swallowed, appalled by how tempting that sounded. Did she really want to be this man's mistress? "And if I don't?"

"You pay back the loan of the rent, plus interest." He pulled out a couple of pristine papers from his attaché. "Here's the payback schedule."

And there it was in black and white, two identical contracts complete with a signatory line and everything. "My," she said softly. "That's thorough." Assuming she got a decent job straight out of school, she would be able to pay this back no problem. Well, not exactly no problem, but it was doable. Very doable.

She swallowed. She never thought she'd be reduced to accepting money from her lover, but then again, she'd found herself doing a lot of stuff differently since filing for divorce. Her schedule was so packed, she was close to the breaking point. Pride would not save her from being thrown out on the street.

Making a swift decision, she pulled out a pen. "I'll take option two," she said as she signed both contracts. "With gratitude." She pushed them back to him and watched him quickly scrawl his name. The letters were neat and precise, including the rapid ticks of a Chinese character, and she found herself enthralled by the elegant play of his fingers. Then he passed her one copy for her records and pushed the second into his attaché.

He straightened and looked at her. She sipped her latte, feeling that she could breathe a little easier. Not a lot easier, but a little. And for that she was grateful. "Thank you," she said. Then she reluctantly pushed the airline voucher back toward him. "I guess I won't need this, then."

He looked down at it, but didn't take it. Instead, he abruptly set his forearms on the table, leaning forward to talk to her quietly but with the same intensity she'd felt when she'd first noticed him across the room.

"Stephen—"

"I never told you what I experienced last night."

She felt her face heat and was excruciatingly aware of Anne watching from the counter. Not to mention Seth and Ethan and Josey. "I don't think now's the time—"

He shifted his hand to lay it on top of hers. He wasn't gripping her. She could have pulled away without a thought. But his warmth and the long play of his fingers kept her still. "Listen just for a moment," he said. "Please."

She nodded. She'd listen. But they didn't need to be sitting there like moonstruck lovers while she did. Especially since they were so very much *not* moonstruck lovers. And yet, as much as she told herself to move her hand back, she just couldn't. She liked it when he touched her.

He must have taken her silence as consent because he started talking. His words were low, barely audible beneath the music playing overhead. But she still heard every one as if he spoke directly to her heart.

"My mother died when I was nine. I remember a little of her. She liked to drink. She had pretty jewelry and nice dresses. If I caught her at the right moment, she would give me a loud kiss and then laugh at the lipstick she left on my cheek." He sighed. "She died in a car accident. Alcohol was definitely involved. Maybe other drugs. I don't know. I was never given the exact details."

"I'm sorry," she whispered. Then she frowned. "You never knew exactly how she died?" If something happened to her mother, she would have to know the details. She would just have to. It wouldn't change anything, but she would need to know. And he seemed like such a precise man, an exacting man. How could he not know?

He shrugged. "I was nine. Details were not given to children. And when I got older, I realized that the details didn't matter."

"Do you miss her?"

He shook his head. "No. That's why the details didn't matter. I have nicer memories of my nannies and the maids. I was told once that she'd married for love, then realized my father wasn't capable of feeling such a thing. Eventually, she just found her fulfillment in jewelry and parties."

"How sad. For both of you."

He shrugged. "It was my reality, for better or worse."

She bit her lip. "I can't imagine it. I just…can't." Nannies. Maids. A cold, socialite mom.

"And then there was my father."

She looked up. His expression wasn't as blank as before. She could see the turbulent emotions in his eyes, which remained trained on the table. He watched his fingers playing with the airline voucher, hitting it against and slightly beneath the coffee cup before pulling it back. He did it again and again while he spoke.

"My father was a good match for my mother. Handsome. Wealthy. A smart man in business, but with a love of society." He fell silent for a moment, and she filled in the gaps.

"As in work hard, play hard?"

"In all the best ways."

She frowned. "I don't think you mean fun-loving, nurturing ways."

His lips curved. "I mean caviar and champagne, limos, gold cuff links, and very, very beautiful women."

"Where did you fit in?"

He shrugged. "I didn't until my fifteenth birthday."

She waited, afraid to guess what was coming.

"My father gave me a night with the Tigress Mother for my birthday. It was to make me a man. After that, I was allowed to join him in his evening entertainments or have the chauffeur take me wherever I wanted to go for my own amusements."

"You became his friend. Sort of a fellow bachelor at fifteen."

He nodded, but didn't speak. He was still playing with that airline voucher.

"Did you know what you…" she began, then stopped. How to ask this question? After all, who was she to say that his childhood wasn't ten times better than hers? It sounded like he had money to burn, women at his beck and call. What guy didn't dream of a life like that? "I grew up here. Middle-class family, Dad's an electrician, Mom cooked and cleaned. One sister married a farmer, the other went techie and works locally on some math/Internet thing. I went to high school, fell madly in love with a football player and married him. We both went to college, but I'm the one who finished. And then it got really unhappy." She shrugged. "Anyway, my parents aren't rich, but we love each other. It wasn't perfect, but it was a family." She bit her lip. How did she ask this? "Did you know there was another way to live? I mean, it doesn't sound like you have a family like I did. Not in the emotional sense." Not in any sense.

He nodded. "I knew. I had friends with a more traditional family. I saw mothers who loved their children, fathers who asked questions about their sons' lives." He shrugged. "I knew. I wanted it. But I had money and tigress women if I wanted to pay for it. And I spent a lot of money on sex."

She winced. "But it wasn't a substitute for loving parents."

"No, it wasn't." He lifted his gaze to look deep into her eyes. She saw vulnerability there. He was waiting for her to judge him, to condemn his childhood or his parents, but she couldn't do that. The man wasn't responsible for how he was raised. And by all accounts, he was doing great—financially and socially—especially when compared to her.

"Different cultures, different values," she finally said. "Who's to say which is better."

"I am," he said softly. "I wanted what you had."

She smiled. "And I want all the money you have." But she wouldn't give up her family for it. Not if she'd had to grow up in an emotional wasteland. She reached out and touched his hand. "What does all this have to do with last night?"

He took a deep breath and his gaze skittered away. Whatever he was about to say, it meant a lot to him. "Last night. I felt. Love." He spoke haltingly, as if he struggled to find the exact words. "It wasn't a sexual kind of love—" He glanced significantly at her. "Though some of that was there, of course. A great deal of that."

She flushed. Good, she hadn't screwed up that part. Especially since she still felt a huge amount of lust for this man. She'd hate for it to be one-sided.

Meanwhile, he continued, still speaking very carefully. "But there was healing love in heaven. My anger faded away." He released a breath. "I didn't realize how heavy that resentment was until it was gone." He raised his gaze to her. "I didn't really understand that I *was* angry. My parents were my parents. Wishing for something different is stupid."

"It's natural to resent it, though. To want what we don't have."

"But I felt it last night. I felt the love that comes when your mother loves you. When you know deep down that you are loved." His hands tightened on hers. She hadn't realized that they were holding hands until his grip firmed. "You gave me that last night, Zoe.

You…we…I was healed. That's what happened to me last night. I was healed. Thanks to you."

She swallowed, overcome by the intensity of his words, his eyes, his entire being. "I didn't— I only—" She swallowed. "It wasn't me, Stephen. I didn't do anything but have sex with you."

He grimaced. "Practice is not sex, Zoe."

She huffed. "I know that, Stephen. But I don't know how to practice. I thought I did, but in the end I just gave up. I did what came naturally." She forced herself to confess. "I did what *I* wanted. It had nothing to do with taking you to heaven. I'd already given up—"

"It worked, Zoe. It worked because of you. Of this I am absolutely, one-hundred-percent certain."

She had no answer to that. She didn't have the power to heal, but…well, the thought was really, really flattering. And so was the way he looked at her: as if she was the answer to the mysteries of the universe. "Stephen…I don't know what to say."

"Then let me talk. You are a tigress, Zoe. Untrained, just beginning, but a tigress nonetheless. Only a tigress could do what you did last night. Please, please do not let your training lapse."

She straightened slightly, her mood souring. All of this was about her continuing to study tantrism? "My MBA comes first."

"Of course. This I understand very well."

There was a dryness in his tone that made her think he had faced similar choices throughout his life. After all, no one ran the kind of business conglomerate that he did by studying tantrism. He had to work sometime.

Meanwhile, he continued to press her. "You have

enormous talent as a tigress. Will you continue to study as time permits?"

She nodded. How could she refuse? Especially if she really had healed him in some way. Plus, it wasn't as if it was hard. Last night had been fantastic.

Then he looked at her and she saw anxiety blossom in his eyes. There was no change in his expression, merely in the tightness of his voice. "Will you, perhaps, continue to study with me? As time permits?"

She didn't hesitate. She didn't want another partner. "Of course I will study with you."

He exhaled, his relief evident.

She frowned. "Did you really think I wanted someone else?"

He shrugged. "You have mentioned problems between us." Then he sighed. "And there will be more problems. Logistical ones." Then he sighed. "I have to go to China. Today."

She blanched. She'd known he had to go back. But she'd thought they had at least a week.

"I have to fire the head of my incubator."

"The banking part. The one that gives out loans to small businesses."

He nodded. "The CEO is a jerk with women. And since most of the people we're helping are women, it's a bit of a problem."

She arched a brow. "He doesn't…um…"

"Molest them? No. He's just a patronizing ass. I didn't realize that when I hired him, of course. And he might have worked out if I had supervised him better. It's really my failure. I hired an ass and so the blame—"

"You made a mistake," she interrupted. "You're human. So fire him and move on."

"Yes," he said, and there was a wealth of frustration in his voice. "I am trying, but it means that I must leave. Today."

She shrugged, trying to make the movement casual, though what she felt was anything but calm. "Well, I have a lot of work to do anyway. Less now that I don't have to worry about covering my rent, but still quite a lot."

"Which is why this is for you." He pushed the airline voucher across the table.

"I can't—" she began, but he forestalled her.

"It was purchased by the Tigress Temple for its newest tigress. A scholarship for study, if you will. You can only do so much this far from Hong Kong. If you wish to continue your studies, you have to make the trip to the temple sometime."

She looked down at it. "The temple paid for it?"

He nodded. "A scholarship. Nothing more."

She picked it up and opened the folder. The voucher was for ten thousand American dollars. "It doesn't cost that much to fly to Hong Kong. It can't."

"It can. But if you use it wisely, you can get two or three trips out of it."

She nodded, slowly convincing herself that it was okay. She wasn't going to be his mistress. She wasn't going to give up everything she wanted for him. This wasn't a payment to a mistress, this was a scholarship to study tantrism. There was nothing immoral or even unusual about that.

"And then there's this." He set a cell phone on the table.

"You cannot tell me that the temple paid for that."

He smiled. "No, that is from me. If I could, I would stay here in frozen Illinois with you, but I have to leave. It is only reasonable that I pay for a phone for you. One that makes international calls so we can talk. So you can continue your studies with me as much as is possible over the phone."

"I doubt there's a whole lot we can do over the phone."

He flashed her a grin. "You'd be surprised."

She raised her eyebrows, intrigued. But before she could ask, his watch started beeping. He looked at the time then cursed in Chinese. She knew before he looked up that he had to leave.

"When will I see you again?" she asked. "Will you be able to come back to Illinois again before the school year ends?"

She saw regret in his eyes and knew his answer before he said it. "I cannot promise. I will try, but…"

"I know. Stuff to do. Chauvinist jerks to fire."

"You have a holiday soon? Thanksgiving?"

She nodded. Her mother usually spent a week beforehand cooking. Her entire extended family gathered for a blowout meal. And that didn't count the smaller parties with neighbors and friends. That's what the holidays were like for her. Dozens of little get-togethers with the people who had surrounded her all her life.

"Can you come then?" he pressed. "Or over Christmas? Hong Kong at Christmastime is a sight to behold."

"I—" She swallowed. "I don't know. I don't even have a passport."

"Get one. Get one today."

"Stephen…"

"Please," he said. Then his alarm went off again. A steady beep-beep that had him cursing again. He stood up. She mirrored his motion and soon found herself gazing straight into his eyes. His hand slid around her back and she arched into his touch. All the smoldering fires inside her blood abruptly burst into life. He was touching her, he was holding her again, and her body remembered all too well exactly what they were capable of doing together.

Then he kissed her. There was urgency in his body, but his lips were almost leisurely as he touched her mouth with his. He stroked across her lips, then teased her by barely slipping his tongue in before pulling it out. Twice. Then a third time, as she stretched up on her toes and wrapped her arms around him.

His hold tightened. Urgency shifted to desperation and the kiss deepened accordingly. He plundered her mouth and she arched into him, opening herself as fully as possible in public. Then she began her own dance with him, teasing and touching as best she could.

She only stopped when she felt the back of her head bump against the fireplace wall. She gasped in pain, breaking away to realize that she'd plastered herself against Stephen from her mouth all the way down to her toes. If she could have wrapped her legs around his waist, she would have. In fact, that was exactly where they had been heading when her head had bumped the fireplace wall.

Predictably, her high-school-aged coworkers were cheering in the background, and she flushed a bright pink. Stephen, too, turned red all the way to his ears.

"Um…" she began.

"I'm going to miss my plane."

She stepped backward, stiffening her spine in determination. "No, you're not. Go fire that man."

"Will I see you at Thanksgiving?"

"Yes." She didn't even think about it. The word was out and she couldn't make herself pull it back. Even though her family—her mother!—would have an absolute fit.

"Thanksgiving, then." He looked at her, one long searching look, before he turned on his heel and rushed out the door.

10

"SO HE'S GONE BACK to China. That sucks." Sarah's quiet voice warmed the large living-room space and helped stabilize Zoe's conflicting emotions.

Zoe smiled in gratitude, but Stephen's absence still felt like a big gaping hole in her chest. "It's just as well. I have a ton of work—"

"There's always work," Sarah said with a sigh as she kicked off her Crocs and stretched out with her feet on the coffee table. Zoe winced at the sight. She'd much rather be seeing Stephen's Italian loafers. "So what are you going to do now?"

"Now?" Zoe shrugged. "The plan doesn't change. I graduate, get a job at a Fortune 500 company, work my way up the ladder, and after years of dedicated effort, I'll finally pay off my student loans." She finished the last of her coffee then stood up with a groan. "Speaking of which, I'm going to recheck my résumé then send it out. The recruiter for Google really seemed to like me."

Sarah looked at her, her dark brown eyes narrowed in thought. "Are you going to call him? Not the recruiter. Stephen."

Zoe knew who she'd meant. "He's still on the plane, probably halfway over the Pacific. Besides, I don't have his number."

"Bet he programmed it into your phone for you. Bet it's even on speed dial."

Zoe bit her lip. Would Stephen have remembered to do that? Was he that thorough? Of course he was. She pulled out her phone. Sure enough, there were the numbers for himself and the Tigress Temple. She smiled, knowing her expression was ridiculously dreamy.

"It is possible to have both, you know—a career *and* a man." Sarah's voice was soft, but her words seemed to echo in the room. Was it possible? Could Zoe have everything she wanted?

No. Zoe just couldn't make herself believe. "Not if he's in China. Besides, I've done the whole marriage thing. I'm not doing it again. I'm not giving up everything I've worked for just for a man."

"Has he asked you to give up anything?"

Zoe sighed, her fears finally crystallizing into something clear and definite. "Stephen's really tempting—in a whole lot of ways—but he's not offering a permanent arrangement and never will. It's better I stay focused on my future."

Sarah nodded. "Just make sure that the future you're grabbing is the one you want."

"I'm sure," Zoe said, then wondered if she'd lied.

An hour later, her résumé was complete, if a little thin. She wanted to be an executive, but her background was full of hourly jobs in every menial capacity possible. Sure, she'd made her way up to manager at the Bread Café—was darned good at it, too—but that wasn't the same thing as working in a salaried position with an international company. No, she was just a glorified bagel counter, and that thought depressed her to no end.

She pulled out her cell phone and began turning it over

and over in her hand. By her count, Stephen would make it back to Hong Kong sometime in the next six hours. He'd be dropping with exhaustion, buried under the avalanche of work he'd avoided while he was here, and too disoriented from jet lag to think of anything but the very next task in front of him. There was no point in trying to call him now. Besides, this phone was really for practice. It wasn't to be used just so she could hear his voice.

She sighed and put the cell phone back down on her desk, only to squeak in alarm when the thing went off. She snatched it up. She hadn't given the number to anyone, so it had to be…

"Hello?"

"Zoe? It's so great to hear your voice."

Stephen! Her heart started hammering triple-time. "Hi there! Where are you? I thought you'd be somewhere over the Pacific right now."

There was a moment's delay and some static, but his voice came through clear enough. "Actually, we're over one of the poles. Can't remember which. But I couldn't stand it any longer. How are you? Did you get the paper done?"

Her knees went weak and she slowly lowered herself to sit on her bed. "You're calling me from the plane? Isn't that expensive?"

"Hmm? Oh. Yeah. But it's on my phone, so it's not going to cost you."

Still. The idea that he—that anyone—would spend that kind of money just to talk to her, filled her with a bizarre warmth. It was just so unreal. And yet, he had done it.

"Zoe? You still there?"

"I'm here. I'm just… It's just great to talk to you. Have you figured out how you're going to fire the jerk?"

"Already done. I had a layover in Chicago and conference-called from there. That was the easy part. Now I'm trying to figure out all the financials. The whole point was to guide small businesses in China, but I don't know what it takes to buy shellfish in Canton or wash hotel laundry in Xian. That was his job!"

"Well, you probably just need water, detergent and a good iron for the laundry. And fish is like any other product with a quick expiration date. Come on, Stephen, you run a multinational pork company. You can handle hotel laundry."

He laughed. "Believe me when I say packaging pork is *not* the same as figuring out the best price for a good iron in Xian."

"No," she said with a smile. "I don't suppose it is." On sudden impulse, she fired up her computer and quickly called up a map of China. She didn't even know where Xian and Canton were, but she was determined to find out. "I wish I were there," she said as she ran her finger over the map of China. "If there's one thing I know how to do, it's find things on the cheap."

She heard him laugh, but it was hard to make out his words over the static. "My vice president...plant..." The rest was lost.

"What? What did you say?"

"—storm. Damn turbulence!"

"What? Stephen!" The static was getting worse and Zoe had to strain to catch even half his words.

"—idea. Can I—not tomorrow?"

"What?"

"—practice. Can't...tomorrow?"

"Sure," she said, even though she had no idea what he was proposing. "When?"

"Be someplace pri—"

"What? Private? When?"

"Yes! —practice long distance. Tuesday?"

Practice long distance? "Stephen?"

"—go—"

"What?" The line went dead, but she still tried. "Stephen? Stephen?" Then she looked at the cell. The window said the call had been lost. She almost threw the phone across the room in fury, but she didn't. It was his only way of contacting her, and no way was she damaging that. If only she knew if he would call tomorrow. And what he intended.

And really, she shouldn't already be getting excited. Damn, it was going to be hard to wait. Harder still to sit through accounting class, wondering if he would call.

She plugged the cell into the charger and got ready for bed. Then she did all the routine things to quiet herself and prepare for sleep. She did her breast circles, she felt the energy flow and she even breathed into silent meditations to quiet her mind.

It didn't work. She kept thinking about Stephen. She kept imagining him in all those places on the map of China. And she wondered what it would be like to be by his side as he tried to search for a cheap commercial-grade iron.

In the end, she gave up. She slipped between her sheets and turned out the light. But she couldn't sleep. On impulse, she picked up the phone and paged through the menu. There it was: the record of his call to her. They had spoken for two minutes and forty-seven seconds. Not even three minutes, but every moment of it consumed her thoughts.

She closed the phone but she didn't put it back on the bedside table. She fell asleep with it tucked tight to her chest.

HE HADN'T CALLED! He hadn't called! Zoe slammed the cash register closed and fumed as she started wiping the counter. It had been two days, and he still hadn't called.

This was exactly why she didn't want to get involved with a man. She'd spaced out in her past two days of classes, snapped at customers, and worst of all, she'd blurted out her Thanksgiving plans to her mother in the most blunt way possible. It had *not* gone over well. Mom did not like her children away for the holidays, especially her unmarried ones. She'd apparently had plans to invite men. A bunch of single men, including ex-husband Marty. As if that alone wouldn't send Zoe screaming for the other side of the world.

But it didn't matter, did it? Because Stephen hadn't called. And when she'd broken down and finally called him, all she'd gotten was the voice mail. And it didn't even have his voice on it! All she'd heard was some damn *female* secretary.

"Wow, if this is what you're like after three days without China-boy, I don't think I want any more shifts with you."

Zoe glanced up at Anne's slow drawl. A cold retort was ready on her lips, but she managed to hold it in. It wasn't Anne's fault that she was bent out of shape over some man. So instead of a nasty retort, Zoe settled for a grimace of disgust.

"Don't worry. I'm off shift in about five minutes.

You're saved for the rest of the day." Honesty made her add, "But I make no promises for tomorrow."

Anne spun around to the room at large. "Who wants my shift tomorrow?"

Zoe felt her lips curve into a small smile. See, she told herself, she didn't need a man to make her smile. All she needed was—

Ah, hell. Marty was walking into the café. This was not, not, not what she wanted!

"Not today, Marty," Zoe snapped. "I'm not in the mood."

"What, am I not rich enough for you anymore?"

She turned to glare at her ex-husband. After all the things she'd paid for? All the money he'd taken from her before and after they were married? Lacking words, she just ignored him, pulling off her apron as she headed to the back. "I'm out of here, Anne," she said wearily.

"Take a cookie, sweetie," Anne said back as she tossed Zoe a piece of chocolate chip heaven. "On me."

Zoe smiled gratefully and headed out the door. Any hope that Marty had gotten the hint died when he sidled up to her as she headed for the bus stop.

"I got my truck," he said. "I could give you a ride?"

"No, thanks. And go away."

"Aw, don't be like that—"

Zoe rounded on her ex. "I don't get paid for another three days, so I don't have anything to steal. Therefore, there's no reason for you to hang around. So go."

His face darkened with fury. "You got a brand-new cell phone. Takes international calls."

Her mother, she thought.

"Do you have the money you owe me?"

"I don't owe you squat. Besides, I thought your new boyfriend was paying for everything."

She threw up her hands. "Where the hell did you hear such crap?"

"Your mother told your sister who told Nick who told me," he snapped.

"And the rumor mill got it wrong. Go figure," she drawled. "It's not what you think."

"We think you're going to Hong Kong over Thanksgiving to be with him. We think he paid for the ticket."

"It's none of your business, Marty," she said as she plopped down on the bus bench.

He dropped down beside her. "I'm worried about you, Zoe. This isn't like you. Why did you sell yourself for a trip to China?"

"I didn't sell myself!" she snapped.

"So, you going to marry him?"

Zoe dropped her head back against the bench and fought the tears. "We're divorced, Marty. You don't get to challenge my choices."

He was silent a moment. Long enough that she opened her eyes to see if he was still there. He was, and his expression was deeply troubled. "This isn't like you, Zoe. You love Thanksgiving. Don't throw your family away over one guy."

"It's a week. One week out of the year." Sure, it was one really great week, but she'd chosen Stephen. "I can see everyone before I go. Or after I come back."

Her bus was lumbering around the corner, so she stood up. Marty glanced to the side, then cursed softly. He dug into his pocket and pulled out a stack of crumpled bills. "Here," he said. "It's everything I have."

She looked down at a wad that must have been close to two hundred dollars. "Marty—"

"I've been a jerk. And I owe you money for my truck. So here, take it. Just remember that even if I'm a jerk sometimes, your family isn't. Don't ditch them just because some rich guy gives you a free trip to China."

"I'm not ditching them—" she began, but he couldn't hear her over the sound of the bus stopping. She just looked at him and his money, doubts piling up in her head. What was she doing? Was Stephen really worth giving up a family holiday?

The bus doors opened, and the driver looked at her expectantly. "Come on, lady. It's cold with the doors open."

Marty was starting to pull back his money, but she managed to nab it before he could change his mind. "I'll take it off your account!" she said. Then she stepped up into the bus.

She found a seat quickly enough, then turned to look out the window. Marty still stood there watching her. His cheeks were turning ruddy from the cold, but he didn't even hunch over. He just stood there watching her like he had when they were kids. Before they'd gotten married, before he'd hurt her, before he'd gotten busted—for the third time—for drunk driving and lost his football scholarship. Before everything bad that had ever happened between them.

He stood there and he watched her with his heart in his eyes. She saw equal parts lust, love and complete neediness that went straight through her common sense and right to her heart. Marty still loved her on some level. And he definitely needed her because he sucked at taking care of himself. Maybe he'd finally learned what she was worth. Maybe he'd finally figured out what he'd thrown away in her. And maybe if he stopped drinking, she could give him another chance....

She closed her eyes and slammed her head backward against the bus seat. That was the very last thing she needed. Reconcile with Marty? That would be like picking up an anchor and jumping into the ocean.

She had a future. She was less than a year away from getting her degree. Then she'd find a job and she'd be able to pay off her tuition debts. After all that, she'd think about a man. But only then! Until that point, Marty and Stephen and any other guy who crossed her path could just go suck an egg. She was busy!

That was her decision, and it felt good! She let out a sigh of relief. She was herself again. No more mooning over a guy. No more—

Her cell phone rang. It took her a moment to fumble it out. She punched the talk button before she could tell herself that she was the new Zoe, the one who didn't run at any man's beck and call. She put the phone to her ear.

"Stephen?" she said, hating that her voice sounded so breathless.

"Zoe! I'm glad I caught you."

"Stephen—"

"Zoe, I've got some bad news."

11

STEPHEN FROWNED at the phone. There was noise well above what he was accustomed to on the other end of the line. And he wanted—needed—to hear every nuance of Zoe's voice. He liked to hear every inflection in her words no matter what she said. And right now, something was interfering with that.

"Where are you?" he asked.

"On a bus going home."

A bus? She rode a bus? Well, of course she did! Champaign wasn't like Hong Kong. She apparently managed just fine using mass transit, though it saddened him that she wasn't surrounded in luxuries.

"Stephen? What's the bad news?" She already sounded defeated, and he cursed under his breath.

"What's wrong, Zoe? Why do you sound like that?"

"I'm on a *bus*," she said with obvious irritation. "There's going to be noise—"

"No," he interrupted. "You. You sound upset."

"Tired. Very tired. And why haven't you called?"

He frowned. "What? I said I'd call today. I told you that."

"No, you didn't. You were going to call two days ago."

He listened for a petulant note in her voice. It was a huge warning sign for him. He was hyperalert for that moment when a woman began to demand things from him, began to make them both miserable when she didn't get what she wanted. Was that what was happening with Zoe? He couldn't tell. She sounded more depressed than peevish, but with all the background noise it was hard to tell.

"I am sorry, Zoe. The connection on the plane was so bad. I am calling on Thursday right when I said I would." He glanced at the clock on his computer. Actually, he was calling a few hours early. It was 3:00 a.m. here, but he couldn't wait until morning. "There has been so much to do here. I just finished my last meeting a couple hours ago." But he'd thought about her constantly. "Did you not get my e-mails?"

"No," she said, her voice softer, and oddly even more dispirited. "Internet's been down at the house and I haven't had time to stop anyway even if you had called. I just thought I'd hear from you on Tuesday."

He grimaced. "I'm sorry if things got confused. Is that why you sound so sad?"

He heard her sigh and his arms actually twitched with the need to hold her. "Run-in with my ex. Schoolwork is getting harder. Everyone thinks I'm a skanky ho. You know, the usual."

"What? A what?"

"Nothing, nothing. I'm just being moody." She took a deep breath. "So what's the bad news? Might as well give it to me while I'm in public. No wrist-slitting allowed on a bus."

He straightened in alarm. "What? No what on a bus?"

He heard her chuckle. "Stop, Stephen! Really, you're too easy. Honest, I'm just teasing. I've had a bad day. That's all."

"Zoe—"

"Stop! Tell me the bad news already. What is it?" There was a steel in her voice that hadn't been there a moment ago, and it reassured him much more than her words.

"I have to go into mainland China," he said.

Silence. Then she drawled, "You gotta help me out here, Stephen. Why is that bad news?"

"Because I wanted to show you Hong Kong. I wanted to take you to the Peak and to Stanley market. Then I wanted to show you all the places tourists don't go, those spots only known by the locals."

"You're canceling the Thanksgiving trip?" She sighed. "It's okay. My mother will be thrilled."

He found he couldn't sit behind his desk, so he pushed up and began pacing his office. "No! No! I was just wondering if you'd like to join me in the interior of China. The paperwork is harder, but I could have my secretary make all the arrangements. We'll get you a visa and everything. But Chong Ching isn't quite the same environment as Hong Kong. It's not so modern. In fact, the places I'll be won't be modern at all."

There was a long pause. He heard background noise and maybe her soft breath. Or maybe that last part was his imagination. Either way, it wasn't enough. He wanted to be there with her!

"Zoe?"

"So the bad news is that I'll need to see you in mainland China, not Hong Kong?"

"Rustic China, Zoe. Very poor China. I will not be able to show you riches."

She chuckled. "I think I'll manage. Stephen, I'm not a world traveler. Mainland China, Hong Kong—it doesn't matter. Wherever you are will be new and different to me."

Relief made his knees go weak. She did not seem to care about the luxuries. "You will need to spend at least a day in the temple. And I'm not exactly sure of my itinerary—"

"Stephen, I've got to get off the bus now. Can I call you back from my room? In fifteen minutes?"

He nodded, then realized she couldn't see him. "Of course. Fifteen minutes. I'll be waiting."

"Bye!"

The line went dead and he slowly snapped his phone shut. He went to drop the phone on his desk, but he didn't want to release it. So he paced irritably about his office, all the while wondering about this new agitation.

Everything was fine. He had a new tigress partner who showed such promise that he could barely believe it. There were practical constraints, but that was nothing new. She was willing to join him during the holidays. She didn't even seem to care that they would be in the country, not the booming metropolis of Hong Kong. In short, everything was great. So why was he pacing his office like a caged animal?

He stopped himself with an effort of will. He had to meditate. He knew it. When anxiety ate his nerves and he had to pace, he needed to clear his head and his thoughts. If he could raise his vibrational rate enough to think, perhaps he would understand his bizarre mood. Unfortunately, the last thing he wanted to do was sit still. He wanted to be in Illinois! He wanted to be home right now preparing for another night with Zoe!

He glared out his window at the lights of Hong Kong. It was the middle of the night. He had the entire building to himself. If any time was conducive to meditation, it would be now. So with a half growl of irritation, he forced himself to sit down on the couch, close his eyes and regulate his breathing. He would find a way to think straight even if it meant sitting here all night!

Her face formed immediately in his mind's eye. Her face, her breasts, her whole delicious body. He remembered her scent, her taste and the feel of her when he was embedded deep inside her.

He spent a wonderful lust-filled minute in memory, then forced himself to empty his mind. He would get no answers while imagining himself kissing her sweet nipples and thrusting between her legs. This was not the way to think!

Unfortunately, she refused to leave. Even when he stopped rutting between her legs, her smile lingered in his mind's eye. Her laugh, her wariness, even the way her blond hair streaked across her face in the wind. Every detail was there in his mind, replayed over and over whether he willed it or not.

And therein lay the problem. He was getting attached. Their work was less about energy and more about her. And that was the fastest way to disaster. He'd seen it before. One partner started falling in "love"— he actually sneered the word in his thoughts—while the other's sights were on heaven. One thought wedding bells and babies, the other meditated on vibrational rates and the kundalini energy core. It ended in disaster every time. And now he was falling into the same trap, setting his sights on his partner rather than on heaven.

Which meant he needed to *stop everything* with Zoe right away. He had to pull his heart away from her and focus back on energy, on practicality, on finding heaven in the most coldly logical way. But he couldn't. She had healed him! Back in Illinois, she had somehow touched the broken, hurt child he'd been and healed him. Even now that quiet peace pervaded him. He was loved. On a deep core level, he felt as if he had a loving parent somewhere. God maybe, or his dead parents. It didn't matter. He was loved, and the joy of that pervaded his every cell.

Zoe had done that for him. And for that alone, he adored her. He couldn't leave her now! He just had to remember to think of heaven, not Zoe. To touch her energy, not her physical breasts. To connect on a spiritual level that had nothing to do with the distraction of the body.

He opened his eyes. He had the answer. He knew what he had to do. And how fortunate it was that they were on separate halves of the world. If only she would—

His cell phone chimed. He still held it in his hand, but the sound jarred him nonetheless. He opened it with fumbling fingers. "Zoe?"

"I'm here. Sorry about that. I realized I had to quiet down before I called you. Had to dump all that negative energy from Marty."

He frowned, wishing for the hundredth time that he could just punch the bastard out of Zoe's life for good. But she would never thank him for doing such a thing. "Do you need help handling him?" he offered, even though he knew what she'd say. "I can—"

"Nah. He's annoying, but manageable."

"Okay." He paused. "Are you comfortable? Is this a good time for you?"

He listened carefully. There was rustling on the other side, but then he heard her huff. "Okay. Shoes off. Door locked. Music on so I don't have to worry about being overheard, assuming I don't start screaming."

He smiled. She didn't seem like a screamer. He set that

as a personal goal for himself, then stopped himself a second later. This was about energy, not about pleasuring her until she screamed his name. Over and over and over.

"I have an idea," he said as he kicked off his own shoes.

"I'm all ears."

"What we practice is a way to excite our energies, right?"

"Yeah. Got that."

"But did you know that energies can touch, even across the world?"

Pause. "We don't actually have to be next to each other?"

He shrugged. "Well, I don't know for certain. It's usually done touching. But theoretically—"

"We could practice across the phone lines."

"Yes." And it would have the added benefit that he would not lose himself in her scent, in her taste, in her body. "If it works, we can build our energies without distraction."

"Tantric phone sex. Hmm." He could hear the interest in her voice. She was intrigued.

"Will you try it with me?"

"Like I'm going to say no to you." Then she laughed and the sound was lighter than before. Freer. And that in turn made him smile.

"You sound better," he said.

"I…" She sighed. "I missed you."

So she was getting attached, too. The thought should not make him smile. Problems got exponentially worse when both partners fell into the physical. It always devolved into mindless sex.

"We need to focus on the energy, Zoe. Our bodies are merely the container. We need to go through them to access the energy, but we should not focus on the container itself."

"Ignore the Tupperware. Focus on the spirit." He could hear the smile in her voice. "Got it."

"Good. Then get undressed."

He heard a catch in her voice. Then a self-conscious laugh. "Naked. Right. Hold on."

He heard her set down the phone. Did he imagine the rustling sounds? He certainly pictured her slipping off her clothes, her jeans sliding slowly down her toned legs. And then, of course, she would pull off her T-shirt, exposing creamy inch after inch of her belly. Did she wear a bra or another cami? He could see both but the end result was the same: high pointed breasts and dusky-rose nipples tight and hard.

"Okay. I'm ready."

So was he. Except, of course, he needed to strip down, too. And turn up the heat in his office, though he doubted he would get all that cold. He stood up, the phone in his hands as he quickly made his adjustments. His office was not really the place to do this—middle of the night or not—but it was all he could manage right then. And location clearly didn't matter to his engorged dragon. He would likely respond to Zoe anyplace, anywhere, anytime.

Stephen sat on the couch, his body already tightening in anticipation. "We should begin with the first forms."

"Breast circles. Got it. Good thing you got this phone with Bluetooth. God bless hands-free headsets."

He grinned, fumbling with his own earpiece as he switched over. Her voice was already rising with excitement. Then he settled onto the couch and set his hand in the familiar finger position on his organ. He hoped she didn't mind heavy breathing. Given his state of arousal, he might just end up sounding like a porn movie.

"Do we do this in tandem? Or should I just start?"

"Tandem. We should describe in detail everything we are doing." Then he closed his eyes and began to settle his breathing. "I am holding my penis in the first position. The strokes will be long and downward at a steady tempo."

He heard her breath hitch, and his mind immediately conjured up her hand on his organ, her body gasping and straining above him.

"Um...my fingers are...um...right by my nipples. They'll be circling outward slowly."

"Exhale on the down stroke." He fitted words to action.

"Inhale on the upward," she said back.

Two strokes later, he realized that things were already out of control.

12

ZOE DID EVERYTHING she could not to giggle. Stephen was taking this very seriously. He took everything very seriously, though she had noticed enough flashes of humor to realize that there was laughter in him, too. She just didn't know if he would be fine with her sense of the ridiculous.

Here she was, playing new-age...what was that? Zither music? Internet radio was a strange and bizarre land. But she had found it and now was sitting naked on her bed doing breast circles while talking to a man in China. At least her life wasn't boring.

Then he laughed. It was muffled, but she heard it nonetheless.

"Stephen?"

"Um. Sorry. It's just rather bizarre to do this in my office. It made me laugh, but I'm—"

"No, no!" she said, releasing her own giggle. "I understand completely!"

There was a moment's pause, but then he spoke and she could hear the smile in his voice. "Of course you understand. There is such lightness in your spirit."

She swallowed, unexpectedly touched. How could he do that? Just one compliment from him and her whole body went molten. "Thank you," she whispered. Then she closed her eyes and focused on her strokes.

"Exhale on the down stroke," she said.

"Inhale on the up," he returned.

She felt her back straighten. Her shoulders rolled back and down, and her neck stretched upward. She felt the energy begin to heat, flowing like a warm stream of peace from her nipples outward.

"That was fast," she murmured, half forgetting that she was on the phone.

"What?" he asked. "What was fast?"

"I'm warming like a Bunsen burner. Two burners, actually," she said with a soft chuckle. "Wow. I am so hot." And she was. She looked at her hands. They weren't glowing red-hot, but they certainly felt as though they were.

"What?" he said. "Already?"

She let her head drop back, exhaling in relief as she stretched her neck in an effort to cool herself. But that lifted her chest farther into her hands.

"I'm switching to the heating circles," she said. "I'll burn off the dross." She wasn't even sure what she was saying. She just didn't want to go slow.

"Zoe? What is happ—uhhhmmm!"

That was a pleased sound, Zoe thought with a smile. Obviously, something was going right for him, too. As for her, she was rolling her head back and forth against the wall while the accelerating circles made her pant. She couldn't just stop at circling her fingers in toward her nipple. She had to finish with a pinch. She moaned in reaction, slowing her movements even further. The next circle ended with her nipples again, but not with a pinch. This time she did a slow lengthening massage. Oh, it felt good.

From the other side of the world, Stephen's gasp

came clearly through the phone. "What are you doing? My chest is on fire!"

"Is it?" she asked. "If I were there, I would lick it. Over your collarbone. Around your pecs. And then I would use my teeth on your nipples. Nip. Nip. Then a soothing swirl with my tongue. Mmm, doesn't that sound nice?"

She made similar movements with her own hands, scratching slightly with her nails to simulate the nips. "What are you doing?" she asked.

"I—I—" He was panting, and the sound was excellent. She didn't know how a sound could be excellent, but his was. "I am trying to control your power, Zoe. You are flooding me!"

Her hands paused. "Is that bad?"

"No—" Another panting breath. "But there is so much! My penis is so full, so hard!"

As soon as he said it, she felt it. Not in her hand, but thrusting up from her groin. It was as if her clit had suddenly grown to mammoth proportions and she widened her legs to accommodate.

"I can feel it," she murmured in shock. "Do a long slow stroke, then circle the tip. Oh, I feel it!" It was as if he was stroking her clit, pulling it taut, and then circling the highly sensitive tip.

"You felt that?" he asked, his voice breathless.

"Do it again."

He did, and she felt her belly tremble from the power of it.

"Let me try something," she said. "Tell me if you feel it." She let her hand trail down her belly and slip into her groin. Tigresses shaved their pubic hair, so as of last night, she was naked down there. The slick, smooth slide over her mound felt sinfully delightful: sensitized, clean and very new. She slipped up and down over it again. "Do you feel that?" she asked.

"No. But we shouldn't expect—"

"How about this?" She pushed her middle finger deep inside her. How she wished it was him. She did it again, tightening her inner muscles around her finger to see if he reacted. "Stephen?"

"My mind is so full. I don't need to—"

"We have to sync more." She reluctantly pulled her hand away. "We need to increase the energy." She returned to stroking her breasts. "I'm doing circles again. Can you feel it?"

"Yes," he murmured. "Not as strongly. I will go back to my strokes."

She closed her eyes and tried to feel her clit as he worked. She thought she caught an echo, but it was fading. "No," she murmured. "We're losing the connection."

"To have done this much is amazing," he said, his breath steadying. He wasn't panting anymore and she missed it.

She concentrated harder on her breast circles, but that just seemed to make it worse. "I think I'm trying too hard."

"Maybe," he said, his voice rich and deep. How had she not noticed how sexy his voice was before this? But then a moment later, she lost the rhythm of his breath beneath another piece of zither music.

"I've got the wrong music on," she snapped with disgust. "Hold on."

She didn't want to leave her bed, but the music was irritating her. Truthfully, she wanted it to be just him and her, but she didn't dare. The walls were paper-thin, and she didn't want to have a screaming orgasm with Janet listening on the opposite side.

She hit her keyboard with irritation, searching for a

different Internet radio station. She ran through pop rock, R&B, even a rap station for the heavy beat, but nothing seemed to fit. And then she landed on sax music and laughed.

"How do you feel about stripteases?" she asked. She meant it as a joke, but the low pulse of the drum resonated with her. And then the sax really kicked in and she closed her eyes, brushing her fingertips across the tops of her breasts at the sound.

All the way across the world, Stephen gasped and she smiled. "You felt that, didn't you?" She didn't wait for an answer, but allowed her fingers to stroke down and across her nipples.

"Do you know what I'm doing now, Stephen?" She straightened up from the desk.

"No," he murmured, "but I can feel your energies growing. Zoe, you are so alive!"

"I'm dancing," she said as she swiveled her hips in time to the music. Then she impulsively opened her dresser drawer and pulled out an ugly paisley scarf her aunt had given her for Christmas. "I've got a silk scarf," she lied. It was actually a very serviceable cotton. "I'm winding it around my neck and down across my breasts. Can you hear the music?"

"I hear you," he said. "I hear the beat of your heart, Zoe. I feel the pulse of your blood through my entire body."

She entwined the scarf around her face and breasts, but it didn't feel right. She had said it was silk and it wasn't, and the lie got between her and the energy. "It's not silk," she said quickly. "It's cotton and abrades my nipples." She tugged it across her breasts and felt the tingles shoot through her.

"If I were there," Stephen said, his voice deep with

a rumbling vibration that settled at the base of her skull—it was almost as if his lips were pressed right there, "I would kiss you wherever the scarf touched. And I would pull it lower and lower on your body."

She let the scarf trail down her body at his words. Given the way her body was still moving with the music, she felt as though she was stripping off her clothes for a dark, mysterious lover.

"It feels so good to dance," she said into the phone. "I took a belly-dancing class once." She arched her arms above her head. "I had to quit because there wasn't enough money, but those first two lessons were amazing."

She let her head drop back as she tried to move her spine in sinuous movements. There was such heat in her body, she felt incredibly flexible. Fluid, even. "I'm dancing," she said with a murmur of surprise. "I'm going to spread my legs and arch backward. If you were here, you'd see everything."

"Pink and perfect and glistening in the light," he returned. "I see it. I'm going to kiss it."

"Use your hand on your penis. Wet the head just like you were wetting me." She let herself fall back on the bed. "Don't worry, I'll feel it." She didn't know where such confidence came from, but she knew it was true.

Stephen didn't answer at first, and she had a panicked moment when she thought she'd lost the connection. Then he spoke, and she felt the rumble of his words lower this time: at the base of her spine and through her back to her core.

"Have you ever done sixty-nine, Zoe?"

She swallowed. "A couple of times."

"Then I want you to think of this. I'm going to spread your legs and tongue you until you scream."

She was already feeling him on the energy projection that was her clit, engorged and tingling with sensitivity. She felt him stretch the hood back, pulling the skin away. And then the rough pad of his thumb circled the whole head. Except she didn't feel it as a rough pad. More like the tiny bite of shimmering light. She tingled on the edge of pain, and she spread her legs wider.

"I want to thrust my dragon into your mouth. I want to push my yang hard into your body while I suck the yin from you. That's what I want to do."

"Yes!" she cried. Her mouth was already on fire. She felt the energy pouring through the back of her throat, setting her tongue ablaze. Even her teeth felt it. Her mouth was alive with him! And down below, she felt a steady draw, a pull and a stretch. The shimmering energy began to pulse, moving slowly about her groin.

"What should I do?" She could barely form words, her mouth was so on fire.

"Draw me in. From above." He was panting. So was she. "Flow out. Below."

She tried to respond, but she hadn't the breath. Without any place to put her hands, she settled them on her breasts, then began massaging them because she wanted to.

"Your nipples," he gasped. "I feel…" He exclaimed something in Chinese, and she would have grinned but she had lost control of her muscles.

The energy was beginning to coalesce into a current. It pushed from her mouth, through her spine, and down to her womb. Her supersized clit began to pulse. It seemed to pull the current lower, deeper. The power went through her womb, then to her clit, burning a path of electricity.

Her clit compressed and stretched. Oh, she could

feel it! Compress. Stretch. Until she erupted in an explosion of power. She screamed in shock, and heard an echo of her cry over the phone. Had he just climaxed? He had to have, because the river of power was flowing. So was she! She was still contracting and contracting! A circle of energy from head through spine and out her clit sizzled through her, and her entire body contorted around it.

The rush was amazing! A circle of ecstasy, she realized, and it kept getting stronger. Her head was thrown back, her body arched, and her legs were spread wide. A white-hot river that wiped her mind and body clean.

Bliss!

STEPHEN WOKE WITH his head pressed to the carpet on his office floor. He felt too weak to breathe, and yet he felt as if his entire body were glowing brilliant white and his mind had never been clearer. His first and his only thought was of Zoe.

"Umm…" He swallowed and forced himself to roll onto his back. He landed with a plop of floppy arms, and he felt a cold wetness on his thighs. He breathed in deeply and forced his mouth to work.

"Zoe!" His jaw was moving. He could speak, though he mourned the loss of light. He hadn't realized how calm and peaceful the glow was until the serenity began to fade. "Zoe? Are you all right."

"Hmm."

He smiled. He'd take that as a yes. So he lay there basking in the same bliss that likely consumed her. It was some time before he felt moved to speak again. And even then, his words were about her. "You are the most amazing woman."

"Wow. Energy sex. It's the way to go. I'm going to love being a tigress."

He didn't answer. He'd had a revelation. Somewhere between the most intensive orgasm of his life and this moment on the floor, he'd realized a terrible truth. But he couldn't give voice to it. Not yet.

"Aw, crap," he heard her say.

"What?"

"Just a moment!" Zoe called, probably to someone outside her room. "Sorry, Stephen. Study group is here. And then I have to make dinner."

"Order pizza," he snapped, stunned by the hard bite to his tone. He consciously softened his reaction. "Stay on the line with me for a little bit longer."

She groaned. "I can hardly move. God, I feel good." Then she chuckled. "But I gotta go. Let me call you in a couple hours."

"Early-morning meeting."

"Jeez, this time-zone thing sucks."

He couldn't agree more. "I want to hold you," he said softly.

"Mmm." He heard a pounding through the phone. Someone was banging on her door. "I'm coming! Sorry, Stephen. I just need to get through this school year. Then job, apartment, and no one asking me to cook." He heard some rustling and a low chuckle that went straight to his groin. "My entire body is sensitized. We have got to keep doing this!"

"Of course," he responded automatically, but his heart wasn't in it the way it used to be. "Zoe—"

"Call me tomorrow, please! As soon as you can!" Then a soft curse. "I'm so sorry, Stephen, but I gotta go." Pause. "Bye."

The line went dead.

His eyes were still closed. He clung as hard as he could to the euphoria of a few moments ago. But the harder he reached for it, the more the feelings faded. And yet, his realization was still excruciatingly clear.

He'd fallen in love with Zoe.

He'd fallen off the energy path and now was focused on a flesh-and-blood woman. All his thoughts centered on her, on her enjoyment, on what she was thinking or doing or feeling. When he'd been stroking himself, he'd been thinking about what he would do to please her. When he should have been concentrating on taking his energy to heaven, he was pouring his power into her. Somehow, Zoe had become more important to him than heaven.

That alone was bad enough, but there was worse on the horizon. If she were any other woman, they could talk about love, marriage, the children she longed for. But Zoe was becoming more of a tigress every day. Tigresses did not fall in love. They did not get married. They did not have children. Tigresses worked with partner after partner, learning more, stretching for the elusive heaven that was so close, but just out of reach.

He knew this because he had done it nearly all his life. And if he didn't have his own experience to draw on, he'd seen countless other women follow that same path at the temple. It was only through his own stupidity that he'd allowed himself to fall off that path.

He'd fallen in love with a tigress. Could he be any more foolish?

13

SHE WAS IN LOVE.

That was Zoe's first thought when she finally saw him at the airport. He looked perfect, his dark suit nicely complemented by the pink roses he held in his hands. And his face brightened like the sun when he spotted her. She, by contrast, felt dirty and rumpled and just plain gross after seventeen hours of airports and planes. And best of all, his first words when she rushed into his arms were:

"Which do you want first? Food, bath or silk sheets?"

Of course she loved him! She would love Genghis Khan if he greeted her that way. This had nothing to do with real love. This was about a considerate man who knew the right thing to say. She buried her nose in the roses and took a deep breath. That and really good sex.

"Bath. Chocolate. Silk."

"Done."

She grinned. "What time is it?"

"Late afternoon. This way." He guided her out to a waiting car complete with a driver in a uniform and hat. He put her suitcase in the trunk, then opened the door for her. He held her hand as she settled onto the seat, then passed her the roses. But he didn't get in the car. Then he looked at her a really long time. She gazed back, but in time, the sights and sounds of the busy airport distracted her.

"Stephen—"

He closed the car door then gave instructions to the driver. It took her a moment to realize that he wasn't getting into the car with her. She frowned.

"Ste—"

"This man will take you to the hotel. It is the best in Chong Ching. Eat whatever you like. Order a massage if you want."

"But what about you?"

"I have to work, Zoe. The business is…" He gave her a weak smile. "It is complicated. I'm sorry. I tried to get everything done before you got here. I have been working night and day."

"I know," she said. He'd told her some of what he faced in his e-mails and on their frequent phone calls. She had just hoped that she would get to see him for more than a moment at the airport. "When will I see you?"

"Tonight. I swear. Tonight as soon as I can."

She nodded as he stepped back from the curb. The car pulled away and she watched him watch her until he was blocked from view. She would have to accept that he wasn't with her. But there were still things to do, an amazing world to see. She started focusing on the sights of Chong Ching, the two rivers that joined in the center, the high-priced hotels and the hawkers who cooked in their woks right on the street! The humid air tasted acrid, the smells very different from cold Illinois. But anyone who saw her smiled and pointed to her blond hair. She found the whole place fascinating. And it continued to be fascinating all the way to the hotel and her suite, and through an exquisite dinner. She found the hotel towels heavenly, especially since they sat on a warmer, and the bamboo slippers quaint. Even Chinese television intrigued her.

But after a few hours of this, she grew bored. She wanted to call Stephen, but didn't want to interrupt him at work. She wanted to sightsee, but didn't want to miss him. Besides, how would she negotiate a city like this alone? And when she did break down and try to contact him, she got nothing but his voice mail. In the end, she fell asleep to a *Friends* rerun dubbed into Chinese. She woke when the door clicked open.

She gasped, pushing bolt upright in bed. Stephen stepped in, his shoulders stooped, his face as haggard as his golden skin could get. "I'm sorry, so sorry," he whispered. "I tried to get away earlier."

"It's all right," she murmured as she rubbed her eyes. She found herself coming awake quickly. "It's fine. What time is it?"

"Three. I didn't mean to wake you."

"Nah. It's late afternoon my time. But you look like you're about to keel over."

He gave her a dry smile and dropped his attaché on the floor. Then his smile warmed considerably. "You look quite good all rumpled like that."

She glanced down. Her faded Is It Friday Yet? T-shirt was scrunched up around her hips, her hair was in her eyes, and her…her breasts were swelling from the intensity of his stare.

"Stephen…" she began, unsure what she wanted to say. Unsure what he wanted her to do.

He held up his hand. "Ten minutes. Give me ten minutes please, and then I swear I'm all yours."

She smiled and gestured to the bathroom. "Take fifteen. But at sixteen, I'm coming in after you."

"Promise?"

She grinned. "Definitely."

He took fourteen minutes. She knew because she watched the clock. In that time, she heard him shave, take a shower and brush his teeth. She didn't think there were hair products involved, but he definitely used the blow dryer. When he emerged wearing the hotel bathrobe, he looked cleaner, fresher, but still had smudges beneath his eyes.

"Now," he said warmly. "What would you like to do?"

Her heart melted. He really was dropping with fatigue, yet here he was asking what she wanted. She grabbed hold of his lapels and pulled him to bed. "Take it off," she ordered as she pushed at his robe.

He arched a brow, but obliged without comment. She watched him move, seeing the way his muscles rippled in the light. He looked leaner than she remembered, more gaunt.

"Have you lost weight?"

He shrugged. "It is hard to find my special herbs here. And I have been too rushed to think much about food."

She continued to look at him, and as she did, his erection grew. He stood there waiting, obviously enjoying watching her watch him. He was a beautiful man, and his thickening arousal was only one of the attractions.

"Zoe, any practice we do tonight will have to be for your benefit. I am afraid that I am too tired to try the ascent to heaven myself."

She grinned. Only Stephen would apologize for being unable to take his own pleasure. She whipped back the covers, inviting him in. He joined her quickly.

"Lie down," she ordered.

He obeyed, settling on his back. She curled into his side, feeling the hard jut of his ribs, the long length of his legs.

"Zoe—"

"Sleep," she ordered. "I've just traveled from the other side of the world. I'm tired," she lied.

He snorted, but wrapped his arm around her shoulders and pulled her tight. Then he pressed a kiss to the top of her head. "Thank you," he whispered. He exhaled, and she felt the tension in his body ease, tension she hadn't even realized was there until she felt his ribs expand and his shoulders slowly sink down into the mattress. His breath steadied, and his knees rolled slightly open, but his fingers weren't idle.

As he relaxed, he traced slow, lazy circles over her shoulder. She smiled, then allowed herself to stretch her hand across his chest. She went slowly at first, unsure of his reaction. But after all they had shared on the phone and in Illinois, she soon grew bold enough to extend her entire arm across him.

He wasn't broad so much as long, and so her fingers quickly reached the opposite ribs. Then she shifted direction and rolled her palm up his chest, skimming lightly over his tightened nipple. She forced herself to stop when she reached his collarbone. He needed to sleep and he wouldn't be able to do that if she was caressing his chest.

Except, of course, he was still tracing a meandering design over her shoulder. Pressed against his side, her nipples were hard and her body was already wet with desire.

"I'm glad you came to China," he murmured. "I have missed you."

"We talked nearly every day."

He rubbed his cheek over her forehead. "I have dreamed about holding you like this."

So had she. This and a dozen other things as well. "Stephen…" she began.

"Hmm?"

"I know you're too tired to practice."

"If you are ready, I can try to help you—"

"No, listen. We're both too tired to do the whole yin/yang energy exchange." She shifted, pushing up on her elbow to look at him. "But the practice doesn't forbid regular sex, does it? I mean, we won't go to heaven or anything, but that's okay, right? It doesn't always have to be—"

"The Tigress Mother would call it a waste of purified ejaculate."

Zoe quirked an eyebrow. "Does that sound as pompous in Chinese as it does in English?"

He grinned. Then he stroked his finger across her lips. "Nothing is ever wasted if it is spent on you."

She sucked his finger into her mouth and coiled her tongue around it. His breath sharpened, and she smiled. She watched him while she toyed with his fingers, liking the way his eyes widened and his nostrils flared.

"So, you up for a waste of sperm?" She coiled her leg up and over his knee. "'Cause I am so ready for you."

He flipped her on her back. She didn't even have time to be surprised. One moment she was on her side, teasing him with her pouty look. The next she was on her back and he was already pressing against her clit.

She arched, her body gasping but oh so willing.

"Still on the pill?" he asked.

"Yes. Still clean?"

"Oh, yes." Then he thrust, deep and hard. She pulled her knees up high to feel him more deeply. He felt so good. *This* felt good.

"Zoe," he murmured as he palmed her breast. The angle was awkward, the rhythm off compared to his steady drive into her. But his fingers were wonderfully naughty as they lifted and rolled her nipple. "Zoe."

Her head was thrown back, her breath short. "Stephen," she echoed, teasing him for saying her name like a prayer. And yet, it wasn't a tease because she loved the sound of her name on his lips. And he was the one deep inside her, angled just the right way to give her clit the pressure she needed. "Oh, you're good, Stephen."

Then she wrapped her legs around him and pulled. His tempo increased. Her belly coiled into an ecstatic pulse. Harder. Hotter. *Harder.*

"Ah!"

The orgasm wasn't heavenly, but it was amazing. Sweet flowing ecstasy that filled her with pleasure. On top of her, he shuddered as well. His hands trembled, his breath stopped, and she felt him pump and pump and pump into her.

She reached up and pulled his face to hers so that she could kiss him everywhere: his lips, his nose, his chin, even his shoulders as he slowly dropped down on top of her. He would have fallen to the side, but she wouldn't allow it. She wanted his weight on her. She liked the feel of him pressing her deep into the mattress and the fullness that came with having him inside her.

"I will crush you," he murmured against her ear. "I do not think I will stay awake long." She would have said something then, but he whispered, "Hold tight." And when she gripped her knees around him, he rolled them over as one. Within a moment, she was the one lying on top of him, and they were still joined.

"Neat trick," she said with a smile.

"Are you comfortable?"

He helped her pull up the covers and adjust a pillow. Their movements were awkward, but neither of them wanted to separate, so they managed.

Zoe pressed a kiss to his chin. "Are you sure I'm not too heavy?"

"You weigh nothing," he said.

What man could be more perfect? She closed her eyes and drifted toward sleep. Her last thought was neither a question nor a worry. It was simply a statement of fact like a warning sign along a road that had to be traveled. She saw it, knew it to be true, but there was absolutely nothing she could do about it.

It read: *China will change your life.*

14

STEPHEN WOKE TO THE sound of a page turning. It didn't hit his conscious mind though. It simply disturbed him enough that other impressions slipped into his thoughts. First and foremost was joy. He was happy, and that made his lips curve into a smile. Second, he realized that he was spooned up against a warm and soft woman. Zoe. His smile widened, and he inhaled deeply. She smelled like vanilla, baby powder and a scent that was all hers.

He tightened his hold, only now realizing that he was hard and she was soft, and that when he pressed his lips to her spine at the base of her neck, she arched in just the right way.

"You're awake," she said in a soft murmur.

"Um-hmm." He lifted his head enough to peer over her shoulder. "What're you reading?"

"A guidebook on China. I tried the Chinese phrase book, but…" She shrugged, which did delightful things to him. "Chinese is hard. Not something I can pick up casually."

His hand slid up her belly, brushing lightly across her breast. She looked over her shoulder at him, her eyes twinkling with a mischievous smile. "Is this practice or just fun?"

Possession. That was the word that flitted through his

mind loud enough to still his hand. What he was doing right now was establishing his possession of her, caveman over cavewoman. It was deep and primal and not at all what he espoused as a dragon master.

He ducked his head, pressing a tender kiss to her shoulder as a way to hide his confusion. But that simply pulled her scent straight into his brain, short-circuiting any higher function.

He rolled her underneath him. She went willingly, and he slid oh so easily inside her. "This is joy," he said truthfully. "Pure joy."

She arched as he began a slow pump, her sigh of delight firing his blood. "Joy. I'm good with that."

He had just captured her nipple between his lips when his cell phone rang. He had forgotten to turn it off last night. His belly tightened for the entirely wrong reasons, and he looked up to see her arching a brow at him.

"Do you answer? Or do you ignore?"

He began sucking on her breast in answer and she gasped. Her knees went up around his hips, her feet twisted behind his buttocks, and Stephen couldn't keep the rhythm slow.

And his phone continued to chime.

He would not answer it! He would enjoy this morning with his…with Zoe. He would take her as a man took a woman and he would have no regrets or thoughts or desires beyond her and this moment. This thrust. This pleasure. This—

The voice mail tone beeped.

He shuddered, forcing his thoughts and his body into order. She was writhing beneath him, clenching him with inner muscles too unsteady to be a natural orgasm. "You have been practicing," he murmured as he felt her contract around his organ, first low then high. Low then high. He raised his eyebrows. "Many tigresses never find control of those muscles."

Zoe grinned. "The instructions said it would drive my partners mad with desire. Is it working?"

He nodded, struggling to keep his breath even. When she tightened around him, he felt as if she were massaging all the vital essence within him, churning it into fuller life, stronger potency, and…and…

He started to thrust harder. He couldn't stop himself. He tried to work a thumb between them, to give her the pleasure she deserved, but she tightened her legs and slammed her pelvis against him.

"Zoe—" he tried, his mind splintering beneath the onslaught of pleasure. He should have prepared himself better. He should have meditated so that he had more control.

"I'm there—already," she panted. "Oh!"

She climaxed around him, and he lost all sanity. Another thrust and he felt his release in a rush that carried all of his spirit with him. She received it—him— and gave back a thousandfold. A tiny energy circle: groin to groin rather than up their spines like before. And yet it was no less powerful and certainly more sweet. And it went on and on.

Until his phone chimed again.

He collapsed on his side with a groan. She chuckled, her laughter like temple wind chimes: light, beautiful and a siren call to more study. Real, meditative tantric study. And yet, he could do none of it while his damn phone continued to chime.

Zoe rolled over to kiss his ear. "Guess I'm not the only one who can't get enough of you today."

"You're the only one I care about."

"Liar," she said with a laugh. She kissed him again, this time closer to his mouth. He snaked an arm around her, intending to pull her closer, but she shoved at his shoulder when the phone rang again.

"I'd break the damn thing if I could reach it." He'd left it all the way across the room, and he'd be damned if he was going to move enough to get it.

She coiled against him, leisurely stroking her foot up his leg. "I love being your partner."

He looked up into her eyes. Did she know? Did she understand how deeply he'd fallen for her? "We weren't practicing just then," he said softly. "And not last night."

She bit her lip. It was already full and plump, and he watched the indent from her white teeth. "Yeah, well, that was just a welcome-to-China thing."

No, it wasn't. At least it hadn't been for him. He closed his eyes. How had his life become so complicated? Except, of course, she wasn't making it complicated. She was giving him exactly what he said he wanted. No ties. Tantric study. But he wasn't sure he wanted that anymore. What if he wanted the earthly path with her? What if he wanted a home and children with her?

Then the phone rang *again*. She laughed at his groan, then rolled off him. "You'd better get that before someone has a coronary. I'm going to take a shower." She jumped out of bed and crossed to his phone, tossing it at him with a flick of her wrist. He didn't even move to catch it. It landed on the mattress and bounced against his arm. Meanwhile, Zoe stood beside her roses, stroking a petal before leaning in to inhale deeply. When she straightened, her eyes were shimmering with unshed tears.

"You're the only man who buys me roses. Thank you." Then she smiled and slipped into the bathroom.

Stephen watched her go, his mind stuttering into silence and his body one big knot of anxiety. He needed to listen to his phone messages. He needed to make some very important business decisions. But all he could think of was a single image: Zoe touching her roses, her expression misty with gratitude, and the way his entire body had swelled because he had made her happy.

If his heart persisted in this emotional aberration, then he would have to give her up as a partner. Hell, he'd already released his sperm—twice!—for no reason except that it felt good. He had carefully hoarded and purified his emissions. According to the ancient texts, he had just shortened his life by two years. He didn't really believe that, but the fact remained that he had done it when he hadn't released in years. He needed to get his tantric practice under control. And that meant no more for-pleasure sex. No more flowers, no more fantasies and no more thoughts of love.

He was not in love with Zoe. And therefore, he would no longer lie in bed mooning over her. He would see to his business commitments. He snatched up his phone and called up his voice mail.

ZOE LET THE HEAT of the shower wash away her thoughts. She was in China. It was the chance of a lifetime. She had just spent an incredible night with an amazing man. So why was she crying?

Because a wonderful man had given her roses? Was she bought so easily? Was she really thinking about changing everything she'd planned because of a dozen roses? She wanted a career, but the dream lingered: a marriage, a home, children. One, two, even a dozen of his kids would be a dream come true.

But it wasn't possible. He wanted a tantric study partner, not a wife. And she damn well wanted a real career. Which meant she ought to be using her time in China to real purpose. Sure, she could be a tourist and look at the sights, but how often would she get the chance to see the inside of a business incubator? One in China? Even if it wasn't a résumé-builder, it would certainly be educational.

With sudden resolution, she slammed off the shower and wrapped herself in a heated towel. This was exactly what she needed, she told herself firmly. Sex was one thing. Career education was something else entirely. It was something productive and important. And roses or not, she was going to do it.

Assuming, of course, that she could convince Stephen to bring her along. They'd talked some about his business problems over the phone. But their discussions had been more about Tantrism than international business conglomerates. Even her travel arrangements had been handed off to his secretary.

He might just be one of those chauvinistic men who had no interest in sharing their work with the little woman, even if she was his sex partner. Especially if she was his sex partner! She didn't know, but she was determined to find out. If nothing else, she knew he would become abruptly less appealing to her if he shut her out of his work. She stepped out of the bathroom while still deciding on the precise tack to take. Did she charm him into letting her tag along? Did she go for direct and just ask? Or did she…

She didn't do anything because he was on the phone

and simultaneously paging through some computer file. His back was to her, his hair rumpled, and his fingers moved quickly over the keys as he whipped off an e-mail.

Then he said a quick goodbye in Chinese. She'd learned that much from the phrase book. He snapped the phone shut before returning to the document. His shoulders were hunched, his chin jutted forward. He had an intensity—or perhaps it was a palpable anger— that told her clearly that there would be no pushing him this day. He was deep in work mode and would not appreciate a tagalong.

She sighed. She hadn't meant it to be loud enough for him to hear, but he spun around. She put on a smile because that's probably what he wanted. "You have to work today, don't you?" she asked.

He nodded, his expression both apologetic and militant at the same time. How did he manage that? "It is a stupid little thing, but it will take a great deal of time. And I…" He shook his head, rubbing his hand across his face before he turned and glared at the computer. "Stupid, stupid."

"I'm sure you'll work it out." How lame was that phrase? Didn't it come straight out of the fifties phrase book? How to please your man and act like a moron in six words or less.

"No, I'm not sure I can. I just…" He abruptly spun around. "Would you like to come with me? Would you like to see…" His voice trailed away in horror. "You want to see the sights instead, don't you? Of course you do. You have never been to China. Why would you want to wander the back roads of lotus-root farms? I'm sorry—"

"Are you freaking kidding me?" she squealed. She couldn't believe he'd just up and offered! "I was trying to figure a way to ask. I mean, it's your business. I didn't think you'd want—"

"You want to go?"

"I'm *dying* to go!"

He smiled, a slow shift in his expression but well worth the wait. Within a minute he was grinning. "Wear clothes that can get dirty," he finally said.

She laughed. "That would be all my clothes, Stephen."

"I will be very fast in the shower." He paused at the doorway to the bathroom. "And if my phone rings again, throw it out the window."

"How about I just turn it off instead?"

"Whatever." He shrugged, but his eyes sparked with a vitality that she hadn't seen from him ever. "So long as I do not have to talk to anyone from the main office in Hong Kong again."

She winced. "That bad?"

He nodded, then he smiled. "I will tell you all about it on the drive out. Perhaps your MBA training can see an answer where I cannot." Then he disappeared into the bathroom.

Zoe stared at the door, feeling her eyes mist and her belly constrict with anguish. How could she not love a guy who offered her dirt roads and challenged her MBA? Oh, God. Was she really falling in love? She couldn't be! That would be stupid. But obviously, her heart wasn't listening.

Which meant what? Clearly she had two choices. One, change her feelings for him. That was looking less likely by the second. Two, tell him. Admit the truth and let the pieces fall where they may. Could she do it? Could she change everything about her relationship with him?

Her thoughts wandered back to last night and this

morning. Her heart softened with emotions that clearly weren't going to change anytime soon. Which meant… she'd have to tell him. By tonight.

She pulled on her clothes with sudden resolve. She'd tell him tonight. For sure.

15

"ZOE LEWIS, I'd like you to meet Mrs. Chen Ai Ren."

Zoe smiled and dipped her head. *"Ni hao ma?"* she asked in her best Mandarin. They were on a dirt track in a village that could not be found on any map. Their car was the only car on the narrow road, and they'd had to maneuver past a water buffalo and three chickens to get to this newly whitewashed home. Mrs. Chen had been in the back, but she stepped out immediately, wiping her hands on a towel as she greeted first Stephen and then Zoe.

"I am well," Mrs. Chen said in stilted English. "You come buy wigs? Finest in all China!"

Zoe laughed, seeing now the display of three wigs on a rack in the single window. "Thank you, no," she answered.

"Ah," said the woman wisely. "You come sell your hair. Beautiful hair! I give you good price!"

Zoe didn't know how to answer. It was a little bizarre to have someone offer to buy her blond hair. In the end, she simply smiled and said, "Not today."

Then the woman laughed back, big and booming, which was extremely infectious, especially given her petite frame. "I tease you!" she said in English. "I know American woman not sell hair! Good joke, yes?"

Zoe grinned. "Good joke!"

Then Stephen stepped forward to explain. "Mrs. Chen was one of our first loan recipients. She borrowed…" He obviously did a quick calculation in his head. "Sixty-five dollars U.S. to buy trinkets."

"Trinkets?" Zoe asked.

Mrs. Chen nodded, then gestured inside. "Come, come and see, *da ren.*"

They followed her into the small shop and then back to the larger work area behind. Zoe turned to Stephen and whispered, *"Da ren?"*

"That is their name for me. It means 'big man.' They know I own the company that loans them money."

She smiled warmly. "Good name."

He shook his head. "Dangerous name. It is a term from pre-Communist China and the origin of the word *Mandarin.* I tried to stop it, but Mrs. Chen began using it because I am tall."

"And the name stuck," Zoe finished for him as they walked into the back working area of the shop.

"See, see!" Mrs. Chen said in English. "Nice hair! Great hair!"

She was right. In the back, a half dozen women worked, cleaning hair in vats or combing long strands to wind into skeins.

Stephen smiled at the vast enterprise, and Zoe would swear he was beaming with pride. "Mrs. Chen learned that there was a wig maker near Chong Ching who bought real hair to make into wigs. So she took that first sixty-five dollars to buy trinkets, which she traded to children."

A young girl of about fifteen stepped forward. She was thin and her eyes were huge, but there was real intelligence behind her sweet smile.

Meanwhile, Stephen continued to explain. "She traded trinkets for the hair in the family brushes. Then she cleans the hair, wraps it into skeins and sells it to the wig maker."

"Good hair! Clean and soft!" Mrs. Chen said. Then she gestured to the girl. "My daughter helps. She counts and checks everything so it is right."

"All on sixty-five dollars?" Zoe said. "That's amazing."

Stephen nodded. "That and a lot of hard work. Her second loan was for a fleet of three bicycles. She hires people to travel to other villages farther out to buy hair." He turned and grinned at the girl. "Mrs. Chen's husband used to drink and then beat her. Now she hires him to bicycle to the northern villages."

Zoe stared at the enterprise around them. The woman had gone from a beaten wife to employer of at least a half dozen women. And if this girl was anything to judge by, the next generation was going to be equally enterprising.

Stephen wandered forward, his eyes keen as he surveyed the working conditions. "Mrs. Chen has applied for another loan." He glanced back at Zoe. "For tuition. She wants to send her daughter to bookkeeping school in Chong Ching."

"Smart girl!" Mrs. Chen said, beaming with pride. "Study hard!"

The girl nodded, the hope shining in her entire body.

"How much money?" Zoe asked.

"About three hundred U.S."

So little! And yet such a class would change this girl's life. She'd have a marketable skill.

"Most of the businesses I've helped are run by women. They could greatly benefit from normal accounting practices, but the male bookkeepers tend to be arrogant and expensive. The women don't like them and the men feel emasculated to be working for a woman."

"But a girl bookkeeper solves that problem." Zoe arched a brow at the girl, who stood silently watching them. "Would she just work for her mother? Or hire out?"

Stephen shrugged. "She would work for me for a while. That's in lieu of interest. And then…" He directed a question to the girl. She answered in quick, confident Chinese. "She said she would hire out to the other women entrepreneurs. Good rates."

Zoe grinned. "Capitalism at its best. This is amazing."

Stephen nodded, but his eyes were on her. "What do you think? Do they deserve the loan?"

Zoe didn't answer at first. This was not her culture, nor was a loan a simple matter. She had no idea how much money Stephen had available or how many other worthy causes there were vying for those dollars. Three hundred wasn't so much money by her standards, but if that same amount of money could start up four other little companies, then why did this girl deserve one scholarship rather than four other businesses?

She glanced at Stephan. "Is the girl smart?"

"I think so. There are a number of bright women in the village."

Zoe pursed her lips. "Has anyone tried to negotiate with this bookkeeping school? If this really is a good possibility, then why not take perhaps four hundred dollars, bring the tutor here, and have him teach ten girls rather than just one? It would probably be safer than sending one girl far away from home. She has to think of food and lodging and the culture shock of going from a one-oxen town to the big city."

"Good answer," Stephen said. "And I know of just the

woman who could help with that." He turned and exchanged more pleasantries with Mrs. Chen before leaving.

Then he guided Zoe down the street to another woman he introduced as Mrs. Hsu. In complete contrast to the hair entrepreneur (as Zoe had now dubbed Mrs. Chen), Mrs. Hsu was haggard in appearance and wore a dirty dress that did not fit her gaunt frame. But worse than that, her head hung down, her shoulders were stooped and she would not meet their gaze no matter how gently Stephen spoke to her. And her daughter—also about fifteen—hid in the shadows with her brother.

"Mrs. Hsu has an extra room. She asked for a loan to buy a bed so that she can rent it out to boarders. Mrs. Chen's hair-processing business has brought extra money into the area. There are occasionally people who come through here looking for a room. She's also an excellent cook and wants to start a hotel."

Zoe smiled, but she met Stephen's gaze with dismay. "There's no way a hotel would survive here," she said softly.

"I know," he answered.

Then Zoe got it. "But she could house a tutor. Is there a large enough space for a classroom?"

He gestured to a large backyard. There was nothing there right now but dirt. But with a few benches, it would provide a great space for a classroom in summer.

"What about in bad weather?" she asked.

Stephen spoke to Mrs. Hsu and she murmured her answer with a weak gesture of a single finger.

"Her neighbor has space. It could be rented for about six cents a day in bad weather."

Zoe nodded. "And that would help out the neighbor as well." She took a deep breath. She got it. She saw now what he was doing. Stephen was singlehandedly vitalizing an entire village, one woman at a time. First Mrs. Chen, then a tutor for the children, someone who would not only help the kids, but provide a business for Mrs. Hsu and her neighbor.

"You've already thought of all this, haven't you?"

He nodded. "I was finalizing things with the tutor yesterday."

Zoe pursed her lips. It would take a lot of effort. "Are they willing to work?" She meant the Hsus. Obviously Mrs. Chen had been, but Mrs. Hsu didn't look as if she could lift a broom, much less convert her backyard into a school.

Stephen smiled. "It is hard to tell. But the first time Mrs. Chen applied for a loan, she had a broken arm and could barely open her mouth to speak. Now she aggressively negotiates terms and is thinking about expanding to a Hong Kong wig seller."

"Your referral, right?"

He grinned. "I am promised a free wig every Christmas in thanks."

Zoe shook her head in amazement. "You are incredible. What you're doing here…incredible."

He smiled, obviously touched by her words. And then he sat down with Mrs. Hsu to talk. A little bit later, the woman sent her daughter to get the neighbor. In time, it was all arranged. And though Mrs. Hsu still didn't raise her head, Zoe caught a flash of a smile on the woman's lips.

It was late afternoon by the time they left the village. They made three more stops, each in locations more remote than this, so that by night both of them were exhausted.

"I'm sorry it went so late—" Stephen began, but Zoe cut him off.

"You astound me. Absolutely astound me."

He blinked. "Why?"

"If I weren't here, would you have slept there? In that last village?" He had certainly eaten the food, primitive though it was. So had she, though it was the strangest food she'd ever seen. And he'd paid for the privilege.

"Yes, I would have slept there," he said as he negotiated the car around a pothole that took up nearly the entire dirt track. "But I forgot to tell you to pack a bag."

"And if I weren't here, you would have slept on a dirt floor with a blanket for a pillow. If you were lucky."

He nodded, his expression wary. "It is the best they can offer."

"I know. I can't believe I ever thought you were snobbish."

He flashed her a wry glance. "I was not at my best when we first met."

"I jumped to a conclusion. I saw your Italian loafers and just assumed you would only eat in five-star restaurants and sleep on a mattress." She looked at him and could barely remember that he had dressed in designer clothing. What she saw now was the kindness in his eyes when he spoke with Mrs. Hsu. And the pride he obviously felt in Mrs. Chen's achievements. "You love helping these people."

He gazed at her. "It is the most rewarding work I have ever done."

She heard the echo of longing in his voice. "But you don't get to do it often, do you? The pork business takes up most of your time."

He grimaced. "It was my great-grandfather's business, but my father turned it into the empire it is today. I am extremely fortunate."

She nodded. "And who wouldn't feel lucky running a pork empire?" She was teasing him, but she knew it wasn't easy. Any multinational business would take a lot of time and great skill. "But you love this here." She waved at a lotus field and a boy leading an ox on the opposite side of the dirt track.

"I have come to hate pork. I don't eat it anymore." His voice was low, but she heard his confession clearly. And her feelings for this man expanded in her chest until she couldn't contain them.

"You're just amazing," she whispered.

It took him a while to maneuver around the huge ox. The creature didn't move quickly despite the way the boy tugged at it. When he finally got past, Stephen drove for a moment in silence, then abruptly slammed on the brakes. They hadn't been moving that fast, but the change still stunned her.

"Stephen?"

He turned to look straight at her. "Come work for me. Run this business for me."

She blinked, stunned by his words. And looking at his face, she saw that he seemed a little startled by them himself, but his eyes remained steady. She almost made a joke of it. She almost forced a laugh and accused him of teasing her. But her words died at his steady look.

"You can't really be offering me a job," she said softly. "You're not that…" Again, she stopped herself. She'd almost said stupid, but that wasn't right. It wasn't stupid to hire her. She'd do a good job, but there were a ton of people who would do a better one.

"I don't speak the language," she said. "I don't know the culture."

"You'd learn the language, wouldn't you?"

She nodded. "I'd try."

"You'd succeed. Plus, with the dialects in the mountains, everyone needs a translator."

She took a breath, still trying to process what he was saying. What he was *offering*.

"Did you see how the women looked at you?" he continued. "The women looked at you with awe."

"That's the blond hair."

"No. It's because you're a small American woman who is not beaten down by her husband or too shy to speak her mind. You are everything they aspire to." Then he shot her a wry glance. "Plus, I think your experience with your ex-husband has taught you something about con artists."

That was certainly true. "But that's not the same as being local. There's so much I wouldn't know the first thing about."

He released a sigh. "True. You'd have to be trained. But I'd have to train anyone I hire. And yes," he interrupted before she could speak, "it was an impulsive offer. But it's an honest one. I think you could do a great job for me."

"I think there are dozens who could do better."

"I've hired dozens. Or at least three or four. It hasn't worked. The men are too arrogant and don't stay around. It is even worse with the women. But you have worked in small businesses. You have waited tables and swept floors and—"

"Done every minimum-wage job available in Illinois? Yeah, but you're talking about running a company."

"Isn't that what you've been going to school to do? Just take a moment and think about it." Then he put the car back into gear and focused on maneuvering around massive potholes.

She leaned back in her seat, studying his profile. The job offer was so tempting. Imagine! Running a business right out of graduate school. But the truth was she wasn't the perfect one for this job. He was. "You should be in charge here, not me."

"I am in charge. But most of my time will be spent at the main office in Hong Kong. Pork doesn't ship itself."

She bit her lip. He'd given her a detailed picture of exactly what his problems were with the larger company. The business was basically solid, but with the world economy in its current fragile state, every dime—or yuen—had to be spent carefully. "But you don't like pork."

He shook her head. "My great-grandfather began this business. His sons will always run it." He shrugged, but she caught the melancholy in his movement. "It is my legacy and I will not abandon it."

She laughed out loud, and his gasp of outrage made her laugh even harder. "My God, Stephen, pork isn't your legacy! Mrs. Chen is your legacy. Mrs. Hsu and whatever children become bookkeepers are your legacy! What you are doing in Hong Kong is just a way to make money so that you can create your legacy here!" She abruptly leaned forward, touching his arm. "Surely you see that."

He didn't answer for a long time. He used the excuse of maneuvering onto a real road to keep from responding to her. But eventually, they started driving down pavement and he had the attention to answer.

"I cannot leave Hong Kong," he finally said. "And I need someone I can trust to run things here." He looked at her, his heart in his eyes. The sight made her gasp. "I don't mind training someone, but it has to be someone I can trust."

She swallowed. Put like that, it did make a lot of sense. But what about… "I would never sleep with my boss, Stephen. Not even if it was practice."

She saw his shoulders slump. She watched his eyes grow distant and then a soft sigh filled the car interior. "So be it. The Tigress Mother would never allow us to continue anyway."

She blinked. He couldn't possibly be saying that he wanted to stop practicing with her. "B-but…" she stammered. "But you've been all over me! You begged me to partner with you!"

He nodded. "And you are the best partner I have ever had. But this company here…" He shook his head. "It means everything to me. I know of no one else better than you."

"I do," she snapped, irritated because she was tempted. "You would be better."

"I will train you. I will teach you everything you need to know, and then I will be assured it is in good hands."

"And then what will you do?" she asked.

"Fulfill my responsibilities to my father and his father and his father."

She shook her head. "This is wrong. You belong here. It's where your heart is."

"I run a multimillion-dollar company in Hong Kong. This is just a hobby to me. A great hobby, to be sure, but it needs someone full-time." He straightened, looking at her with a calmness that stunned her. "It is a real job offer, Zoe. I trust you. I *need* you. Will you come?"

She swallowed. She couldn't believe the opportunity, the possibility. It didn't make sense. But ridiculous as it was, she couldn't afford not to take the chance. Even if it meant she was going to live in freaking China!

"I'm not the person for this job."

"Let me be the judge of that."

She took a deep breath. Career or sex? Career or a confession of love to someone who clearly wasn't in love with her? Career or guaranteed eventual heart-break? Put like that, the answer was obvious.

"Yes," she said before she could change her mind. "Yes, I'd love this job."

16

SHE'D NEVER WORKED harder during any holiday. In fact, she didn't even remember that it was Thanksgiving until Stephen served her a plate of turkey over the spreadsheet she was studying. She blinked up at him in surprise.

"Happy Thanksgiving," he said.

"Where did you get this in the middle of China?" She took a bite of stuffing. It was…unique. She'd never before had turkey stuffing with soy sauce in it.

"We're not a completely backward country, you know. We have chefs."

She gestured to his plate of dumplings. "Then why aren't you having any?"

He laughed. "Are you kidding? Turkey in China? I can only imagine how bizarre that must taste."

She nodded, then leaned back in their tiny office space. "I didn't even remember it was Thursday."

"You've been working hard," he said, his tone carefully neutral.

She looked at him, and when she spoke the shock in her voice was as much for him as for her. "I can't believe how…fabulous this is. Stephen, I want this job so bad I can taste it."

He arched his brow. "You already have the job, you know. You don't have to—"

"I thought you would come to your senses. But, Stephen…" She looked around the tiny office space. It had the bare necessities: a desk with his laptop on it, a single computer and printer—both outdated by American standards—a front reception area that was simply another desk covered with documents, all written by hand. They were on the outskirts of Chong Ching, but clearly in the low-rent district.

"This is night and day from what I'd imagined myself doing," she said. "I pictured sleek glass and metal, a high-rise building with climate control, and a cubicle of some kind. I never thought…China."

He didn't respond. She looked up at him, seeing his carefully neutral expression, and her heart twisted within her. They'd been working around the clock as he tried to train her in the details of the small businesses he supported. They had been all over this part of China by car, by bike and even once on foot beside a boy and his water buffalo. She now understood the logic of his job offer to her. He actually had enough local talent for the mundane details of the business, people he'd sponsored or trained now working off their interest to him in services rendered.

What he didn't have was a trustworthy person of vision to run it all, to think beyond the obvious, to dig deeper and quickly spot ways to support the new entrepreneurs. He needed someone who understood business and people both.

That person could be her. She so wanted it to be her. If only the job didn't come with a cost. A huge, freaking mega-cost.

She had to give him up. She wouldn't be both his lover and his employee. She'd already seen that there was a lot to learn, a lot to master. She would be proving her worth on a daily basis, not only to Stephen but to every person who applied for a loan, who took Stephen's money and tried to make a business work. She couldn't possibly afford to be viewed as his mistress.

He knew it, too, and so had moved out of their shared hotel room. She hadn't even noticed it until he'd escorted her to the suite and then left her at the door without so much as a goodbye kiss. They'd both been dropping from fatigue, so she hadn't argued. Besides, she knew he was right.

But the pain of it still created a cold ache in her chest whenever she looked at him. She'd been about to tell him she loved him. But she wanted this job! Why did she have to lose him to have it?

He passed her another spreadsheet. "We leave for Hong Kong early tomorrow," he said, his tone still neutral. "Can you be ready by six?"

She nodded, her thoughts distracted as she flipped between one spreadsheet and the next. "I'd really rather spend the rest of my time here," she said neutrally. "What's the penalty if we change the reservation?"

He didn't answer. In fact, he was silent so long that she had to look up to see if he'd heard her. Apparently, he'd been waiting for her to give him her full attention.

"Stephen?"

"You must go to the temple, Zoe. You are a tigress, whether you know it or not. You should not let such a thing fade from lack of attention."

She winced and looked back down at the papers in front of her, though she didn't actually see any of the neat columns of numbers. "I don't want a new partner," she said softly. "I don't know that I can do what we… I don't know that I can study with anyone else."

"Then study by yourself," he answered. "You don't need to take a partner right away."

She shook her head. It wouldn't mean anything without him. She didn't even want to talk about Tantrism with anyone else. Her eyes were filling with tears at just the thought. Then she felt his hand beneath her chin, firm and steady as he slowly pulled her head up to face him.

"There is always attachment with one's first partner."

She swallowed. *Attachment* was such a tame word for what she felt for him.

He must have seen the flicker of emotion in her face because his expression grew tortured. "Please do not make this harder, Zoe."

"Why would the Tigress Mother separate us?" she said.

"What?" He frowned, but she would swear it was an affectation. He knew exactly what she had asked, but he was trying to delay answering. She didn't give him that luxury.

"You said before—when you offered me the job— that the Tigress Mother wouldn't allow us to continue as partners anyway. Why? Why would she separate us?"

"You would work here and still partner with me?" he rasped.

Her gaze slipped away. "No," she said softly. "I can't. You know I can't."

He nodded. "And neither can I." Then he abruptly tilted his head down. The movement was swift, but she saw it coming and she lifted her face to him.

His tongue teased the seam of her lips even as she opened for him. He did not press inside but spent long moments nipping and caressing the edges of her mouth. Soon, she was the one who reached up and wrapped her arms around his shoulders. She was the one who deepened the kiss, fusing her mouth with his.

He met her fire with his own desire. Their tongues danced, their bodies pressed tight to one another, but in the end, they both pulled slowly back. She was breathing hard, and her hands trembled from the force of will it took to step away from him. She didn't want to be separated by even so much as a breath of air. And yet, she knew it wasn't possible. Not if she wanted this job. And, oh, how she wanted the job.

"Stephen..." she began.

His lips curved in a rueful smile, but his words said nothing about the longing she saw in his eyes. "Eat your turkey, Tigress Zoe. I have some phone calls to make, and then I will take you back to your hotel."

She opened her mouth to argue, but she didn't know what she could say. What if she blurted out, *I love you?* What if...

She held it back. If she wanted this job, she had to keep her mouth *shut.* No kisses. No confessions. So she nodded and dutifully picked up her fork. He gave her one final lingering look before he opened his cell and stepped out of the tiny office.

THE TIGRESS TEMPLE was everything she'd imagined and more—beautiful, remote and wonderfully exotic. Zoe endured an hour-long meeting with the Tigress Mother, who was beautiful and cold. The woman outlined a course of study for Zoe to pursue alone, then indicated that a new partner could be found for her in Chong Ching.

Zoe didn't argue. She was too dazed and too sick at heart. She collected the texts, sat in on a few classes and spent the night in a room that managed to feel like sex even though it was simple and clean, and Zoe did nothing more there than change into her pajamas and sleep. In the morning, the temple chef drove her to the airport. Apparently, Stephen had been called away to meet with his VP and could not get away. He had, however, left a silk scarf for her.

She cried into the soft fabric during the entire long trip home.

17

ZOE WAS BLEARY-EYED when she arrived in Champaign. It was dark outside, but she didn't really know whether it was early morning or late evening. Jet lag was a killer. Thankfully, she didn't have to get a ride home. Her mother was going to…

Her mother wasn't there. Marty stood at the base of the escalator, a big smile of relief on his face when she appeared. Zoe sighed and wrapped her silk scarf around her neck.

"He give you that?" Marty asked as soon as she stepped off the escalator.

"What are you doing here, Marty? Where's my mom?"

"She asked me to get you. She wants me to bring you right home. Says she's got a big slice of pecan pie for you."

Zoe shook her head. She loved her mother's pie, but she just couldn't face her family yet. She didn't know what she would tell them. How exactly did she break the news that she was going to live on the opposite side of the world? And how did she explain that she was really excited about her job when she felt so freaking miserable?

"I can't tonight, Marty. I'm too wiped."

"We're worried about you, Zoe."

She arched a brow. "You're worried about your

gravy train. Well, sorry, Marty, that train left the station a long time ago."

"That's not fair!" he snapped, his expression darkening. "Yeah, I was a jerk, but we had a life together. I've got a steady job now, and I'm doing good. And…" He dug a crumpled twenty out of his pocket. "Here's another installment on what I owe you."

She took the money and slipped it into her pocket, doing the mental calculations while they moved to the luggage area. But when she looked at Marty, a shock reverberated through her system.

She didn't love him anymore. And more important, she didn't hate him, either. What she felt for him was a sweet nostalgia for what might have been, much like what she felt for a dollhouse she'd once created out of cardboard boxes or that big fort she'd nearly finished in her backyard. Marty was like an ambitious childhood project—one that could have been awesome, but for one reason or another never got finished.

"Thanks for the money, Marty. And the ride home."

He narrowed his eyes, obviously thrown by her attitude. So was she, actually. It was odd to speak polite banalities to him without any of the emotional overtones. It was freeing, but weirdly so.

"You're different," he said softly.

"In a good way, I hope."

He shook his head. "Nope. In a brainwashed way."

She smiled. She almost patted him on the head for being so cute. Instead, she leaned down and pulled her luggage off the carousel.

"Um, here. I'll get it." He took it from her hand and rolled it toward the door.

He might have lifted it off the rack for her, she

thought sourly, but whatever. She followed him out into the biting wind. His truck was parked illegally in a handicapped spot, but she didn't comment. She just climbed into the cab as soon as he unlocked it and was grateful to be out of the cold. She heard her luggage drop into the back, and then Marty scrambled into the driver's seat.

"It's too cold for that scarf," he said.

She didn't say anything. But she did gather the silk close and brush her cheek against it. Stephen's fingers felt like that sometimes. Soft, tender. Excruciatingly sweet.

She missed him. She didn't know how she'd work with the man and not remember, not *want* something different. But it was like her dream of babies and picket fences. She was making a career for herself, a future that she could be proud of. No woman could do it all, and she would sacrifice one dream for the reality of a career. And she would not regret it. Or so she told herself over and over and over.

"I've accepted a job offer," she said, finally forcing herself to say the words out loud. In this way, she committed herself wholeheartedly to her future. "Right after graduation, I'm going to work in China. It's a great opportunity, and I'm really excited." She turned to see Marty staring at her in openmouthed shock. She smiled. "It's such a big world out there, and I want to do big things."

"Don't be ridiculous. You're a small-town American girl."

"Champaign isn't all that small." Certainly not in comparison to the villages she had seen.

"You are not capable of working in China, for God's sake!"

She bit her lip, blinking away the tears. So, okay,

Marty still had the power to hurt her, but not because he didn't believe in her. That was old news. He was echoing the very doubts she had been whispering to herself. She didn't say anything as he shifted the truck into gear.

"You don't even speak Chinese!" he snapped.

"I'll learn."

He rolled his eyes, and she turned away to stare at the dark landscape. They were passing cornfields and the railroad tracks. She frowned. "My house is the other way, Marty."

He didn't speak, but kept his face resolutely forward.

"I don't want to go to my parents."

His only answer was to clench his jaw. Then she looked harder. They weren't headed to her parents, either.

"Where are we going, Marty?" She straightened, truly alarmed. "Marty, where are you taking me?"

He looked at her then, his eyes cold and his expression…regretful? It was the way he looked when he was about to confess something. When he'd wrecked her car or drunk his last paycheck. "I told you, you're brainwashed."

"I… What? Are you kidding me?"

His bottom lip stiffened. "It's for your own good, Zoe. Your mom thinks so, too."

"That anyone who falls out of love with you is brainwashed?" She could *not* believe this!

"You missed Thanksgiving. You're carrying around a scarf like it's holy. You don't even like silk! You said it's too impractical."

"That's bullshit, Marty! I like silk just fine. It's only impractical when you don't have the money for food or rent."

He turned his face back to the road. "This is for your own good."

"You are fricking insane! Take me to my parents right now!" She figured she'd have a better chance to get to her parents' home than to her own apartment.

He smiled. "See, I knew this would work. You're already coming out of it. You want to see your family."

Shock made her jaw go slack. Was he really that delusional? She took a deep breath and spoke slowly, soothingly. "Marty, you're really freaking me out right now. Please just take me to my mother, okay? You like my mom."

He nodded. "She's great. And not yet, Zoe. You're not quite ready yet." Then he turned his attention back to the road as he accelerated onto the freeway.

STEPHEN TWIRLED HIS pen as Jiao Kai put a stack of papers on his desk. They were important papers, yet another report that was vital for him to understand. He needed to see beneath and behind the numbers before he made a decision that could affect the entire future of pork products.

He was thinking about roses instead. Dark red roses. Lighter platinum roses. Even the odd orange-striped roses that reminded him of sherbet. He'd wanted to give Zoe more roses. He wanted to see her eyes light up and watch the way she'd always bury her face in the blossoms first, then twist away so that the petals brushed across her cheek. Once, she'd even pulled the bloom slowly over her lips, and he was abruptly rock-hard at the memory.

"Stephen! Do you understand?"

He nodded without even thinking. He understood. He understood that he was going to be chained to this desk inside this high-rise office for the rest of his life. That he would wake every morning to more reports just like this one. And no matter how hard he worked during the day, he would still return in the morning to find more on his desk the next day.

It was, after all, the lifeblood of his company—these numbers that represented pigs or distribution nodes or vacation-time allotments. Hell, he even had a huge folder on insurance policies to cover industrial accidents in the event of world economic collapse or something. His lips curved in a smile. It would take a world economic collapse for him to escape this room.

Or one blond woman who could smile at him and cut straight to his heart. He glanced at a clock. She was just now boarding her plane to return to the United States. Would she wear the silk scarf he had left for her? Would she think of him as it touched her skin?

"You belong here in Chong Ching," she'd said. "You should be running this company, not me."

She was right. He'd known it then. He knew it now. But how?

"Stephen!" Jiao Kai snapped.

He looked up. "You've done a good job," he said, seeing the man before him. If anyone lived and breathed pig futures, it was Jiao Kai. He wasn't perfect as a leader. He didn't have the charisma of a multimillion-dollar CEO. Stephen couldn't remember the last time the man had smiled. But he had a head for pigs, packaging and distribution nodes. And the only reason Stephen made sense of the reports was because Jiao Kai brought the damn things to his attention.

"I think I'm going to promote you," Stephen said rather casually. It wasn't a conscious decision so much as a shift in reality. A shift to what was *right*.

Jiao Kai blinked. "Do you wish more coffee? I do not think you are fully awake yet. And there is a great deal more to discuss."

Stephen shuddered. "No, no, there isn't." He closed his eyes. Her face appeared immediately. Blond hair, blue eyes and lips that curved mischievously even while her mind cataloged and processed everything around her. In that small way—in her brilliance and steady hard work—she absolutely reminded him of Jiao Kai.

"I offer you the position of CEO," Stephen said. "And a thirty-percent raise." He was being a canny negotiator. The man actually deserved double his current salary. But the world hog market wasn't what it used to be.

Jiao Kai stared, his mouth dropping open in shock. "But…what will you do?"

Stephen laughed. His mind was on Zoe, his eyes drifting to his office couch. She had never been in this office, but her spirit had. He had been sitting on that couch when they'd first bonded, mind to mind, on the phone.

Except, of course, he wasn't going to be with her. He was, in fact, going to *steal* her job from her. The very job he had just offered her and had worked for a week to convince her to take. But he needed that work. He needed to run that company.

"I still have my stock and my seat on the board. Don't think I'm going to be unemployed." Or poor. Assuming Jiao Kai ran things well, he was still going to be a wealthy man.

"But—"

"Two minutes, Jiao Kai. You have that long to decide."

"Fifty percent increase in salary."

Stephen arched his brow. "Thirty."

"Thirty-five."

"Done." Stephen punched the button to reach his secretary. "Book me on the next flight to the States." With luck, he would only be a few hours behind her.

ZOE CAME SLOWLY awake. She was cold and... She sneezed. Damn. It hadn't been a nightmare. She was in an old barn. A barn! And sleeping on a moldy mattress beneath a blanket scratchy from hay.

She glared at Marty as he stretched out snoring in a sleeping bag on an air mattress. She'd had the option of sharing the comfy sleeping bag with him, but had opted for scratchy hay and mold instead. God, was anything more ridiculous?

She pushed silently to her feet. It wasn't ideal, but she could sneak out now. Marty had his truck keys clutched tightly in his fist, so driving was out. But she could walk somewhere even though he'd taken her shoes.

Last night she'd tried to reason with him. He'd driven them to the barn, parking his truck all the way inside. Then he'd gotten out his hunting rifle and ordered her out on the promise that they'd just talk for a while. She'd agreed because she stupidly believed logic could still reach him, even with the rifle. But logic didn't have a prayer of penetrating his massive male ego. Certainly not after he'd guzzled the first beer. He seemed to think everything she'd done—the divorce, graduate school, even her trip to China—was in reaction to the dissolution of their marriage. As if her life was dependent on him.

The ego of that belief was beyond reason. And even if she knew his ego needed the lie, she couldn't allow him to stop her just because his identity was still wrapped up in her.

So she'd tried to talk to him. She'd ordered, cajoled,

reasoned and pleaded. She wasn't afraid until he'd held her down and stripped off her shoes. Her sneakers were now hidden somewhere in his bedroll.

He hadn't hurt her beyond that. She had one hell of a bruise on her collarbone where he'd held her down. He had a few new bruises, too, but they hadn't been enough to change his mind about keeping her trapped in this stupid barn.

In the end, she'd settled in to wait. Eventually he'd fallen asleep, especially after the six-pack was gone. But she'd had to pretend to doze off first before he relaxed enough to sleep on his own. Which would have worked if she hadn't actually slept. But now she was awake and he wasn't, so it was time for her to escape.

She pushed to her feet, wincing as a rock cut through her thin sock. Damn, the ground was cold. How long before someone came looking for her? A day, at most. Unless her mother really was helping him. Mama always did have a soft spot for Marty.

She made it halfway across the barn. Far enough to pick up speed. Far enough to think she might have a chance. Far enough that Marty built up a hell of a lot of momentum as he tackled her.

She hit the ground with an *umph!* Her head bounced painfully in the dirt and her neck snapped back. She cried out, kicking blindly with all of her strength. But Marty had been a football player. There wasn't a damn thing she could do to him to make him let go.

"Zoe, stop!" he grunted. "Damn it! You're only hurting yourself."

He was right. And besides, he had her pinned now, facedown in the dirt, his erection thickening against her backside. That realization alone made her still.

"I give, Marty," she said softly. "Get off."

"You won't run?"

She swallowed. "I'd never make it anyway."

"True, that."

"So get off."

He held her pinned a little longer, and she feared he'd choose the darker option. He'd always liked their sex a little rough. But in the end, he pushed up and off her. She shuddered as she rolled into a seated position, tucking her knees up to her chin.

Marty looked down at her and cursed. "Jesus, Zoe. Don't look at me like that. I'm not going to hurt you. I'm not a monster."

"Then let me go. I've got classes."

He shook his head. "This is more important than school. Damn it, Zoe, what's gotten into you? China? Do you seriously think he's going to give you a *job* in China? You'll be stripped naked and sold in the nearest brothel!"

She gaped at him. "Stephen is not a white slaver."

"How the hell would you know that? It's not like they advertise! I mean, come on. Think about it! A rich Chinese guy comes in, buys you a ton of gifts and sweeps you off to China. It's not real, Zoe. Life just doesn't work that way."

She shifted onto her knees, pressing her hands to the ground so she could spring to her feet at a moment's notice. "I'm not in China, Marty. And the only one who's abducted me is you." She looked around the barn. "What's your plan here, Marty? You going to hold me here until I promise to take a job in America? Did you think we were going to get remarried? Live happily ever after? Because you *abducted* me?"

He rubbed a hand over his face. "I just want to talk to you."

"So talk." She pushed to her feet, reassured when he didn't slam her back down on the ground. But he wasn't exactly giving her back her shoes, either.

"Give me a minute!" he huffed. "You know I don't think well without food."

"Give me back my shoes."

He shook his head. Then he got a sly look. "I got something better."

"I doubt it," she drawled. But then he held out a granola bar and her stomach grumbled. She hadn't eaten since somewhere over one of the poles. But she didn't reach for it. That would mean stepping closer to Marty, and she didn't trust him that much anymore.

He read the wariness in her expression and cursed again. "Jesus, it's not poisoned." Then he threw it at her feet.

She reached down and picked it up slowly while he pulled open his own and bit off a hunk. And so they passed another hour: eating, staring and not talking. Eventually, Zoe lost her temper.

"I'm bored, Marty, and I need to pee. Let's just go to Mom's and—"

"We've been camping before." He reached into his truck and tossed her a roll of toilet paper. "Use the corner over there."

She caught the roll and stared at him, lining up facts in her mind. Bedroll and mattress, at least two granola bars and now toilet paper. Not to mention access to this barn. "You've been planning this for a while."

He shrugged. "Everything went wrong the day you left me."

She snorted. "Everything went wrong long before that." Typically, he refused to hear her. Which meant she had to think of a new strategy. But first things first. She crossed to the corner where he'd dug a hole for her use. Great, just great. And she'd thought China was primitive. At least they had outhouses.

No chance of escape right here. She was blocked in the corner between two walls. She took her time as she unzipped her pants. She needed to think. How could she get help? Marty had her purse and cell phone. She'd already tried screaming last night, but Marty had assured her that no one came anywhere within a three-mile radius of here. Which meant…

She'd connected psychically with Stephen before. True, they'd been on the phone and engaged in something designed to make them connect. But it was her only thought right then. She closed her eyes and tried to concentrate.

"Hurry up!" Marty called from behind her. "You always did take way too long in the bathroom."

"Bullshit," she muttered, but that was Marty through and through. Always willing to rewrite history to fit his version of reality.

"Zoe—"

"I'm coming!" she snapped. "Give me a minute."

He gave her about thirty seconds. It was all she needed. In fact it had taken her only twenty seconds to realize that no way, no how was she making some psychic connection with Stephen. First, she wasn't in the mood. Second, he wasn't even aware that she was trying to reach him. Third, and most important, he was on the other side of the freaking world. Even if he did get her message of I'm-in-trouble! what was he going to do about it? Probably call her cell phone. And when she didn't answer, he would probably assume that she was in class. It would be a day or more before he started putting the pieces together.

In short, she could not look for any rescue from him. She zipped up her pants, grateful for the return of warmth. Then she sighed and headed back toward Marty. She would just have to think of something else. But what?

18

MARTY WAS ON HIS second granola bar when the cops broke through the barn door. He was so frightened that he dropped the bar and promptly wet himself. The rifle landed beside his food, and then he got a really close look at both as he was shoved face-first into the dirt.

It was over by the time Zoe had enough breath to think about screaming. And by then an officer was wrapping his jacket around her and asking her if she required medical attention.

"Um, no," she murmured, still dazed by the sight of Marty with his hands linked behind his head while three cops pointed their guns at him. "How'd you find us?"

She had an irrational moment thinking that her psychic scream to Stephen had made it through before her mother came running in the open barn door, gasping, sobbing and spitting angry curses at Marty. She ran straight to Zoe, crying, "Are you all right? Oh, my God, are you all right?"

"I'm fine, Mom. He didn't hurt me."

"I can't believe this! That Marty…of all people! Oh, Zoe, are you sure you're okay?"

"I'm fine, Mom. I'm fine. How'd you know…" Her voice trailed away as she saw someone else walk in. Someone tall with dark Chinese hair and a drawn face.

Zoe had to blink to make sure she wasn't seeing things. She wasn't. It was Stephen, looking more pale and rumpled than she'd seen him before.

Her mom must have seen the shock on her face because she started answering questions Zoe hadn't had the breath to ask. "He stopped by your place and couldn't find you. Then he came by our house, and you hadn't come by last night. And idiot there didn't show up for his shift at the bowling alley. Then we went to his place and found a list of supplies plus books on deprogramming. Honestly, what a moron! Are you sure he didn't hurt you?"

Zoe blinked, struggling to believe that Stephen was really here, rescuing her in Illinois.

"Are you all right?" His voice was low and yet it vibrated through the air straight to her heart.

She nodded. "Why are you here?"

He didn't answer except to reach her side and wrap her in his arms. She buried her face in his chest, at last allowing herself to relax, to let her fears and anxiety release. They drained away into him, and he accepted the burden easily. His body was rock-solid, his breath warm, and she never, ever wanted to leave his arms again.

"You're here," she whispered. That was all that mattered.

He pressed a kiss to the top of her head, and when he spoke, the words rumbled from his body into hers. "I had to see you. You'd been gone for just a few hours when I realized I had it all wrong. I changed my flight and got here as soon as I could. I have to tell you something."

But he didn't continue. He didn't explain because this was obviously not the time. With her mother here, plus the cops, and Marty cursing up a blue streak as he was led out in handcuffs, they couldn't begin to have a serious conversation. Which meant she had to get through this before she would know the truth. But the questions still lingered in her mind. Why was he here? What did he need to say? The possible explanations made her heart beat triple-time and her mind spin with anxiety.

He didn't leave her side. He wrapped his arm around her shoulders and stood there as a solid source of strength while she gave her statement to the police. They insisted she go to a hospital just to be checked over, and the whole process took hours, but he never left her. And when it was done, he took her hand and led her to a rental car. Her mother had tried to insist that she come home, but Zoe had refused. She wanted a shower. She wanted her own bed. But most of all, she wanted some privacy with Stephen. So she promised to see her mother tomorrow, and then gratefully allowed Stephen to drive her wherever he willed.

He took her to Café Paradiso.

"Is this all right?" he asked as they pulled in to the parking lot. "I thought you might want some food and quiet before seeing your housemates."

She groaned at the thought of all the fuss her friends would make the moment she walked in the door. They knew she was safe; her mother had already contacted them, but the last thing she needed was to face more well-meaning attention. She only wanted Stephen right then. Just Stephen.

"It's perfect," she said. "Absolutely perfect."

He got her a mocha and her favorite sticky bun. And then finally, blessedly, they were alone in a booth and she could ask the questions that had been circling through her brain since the moment she'd seen him in the barn.

Except that the words didn't come. Nothing came except for the caress of his hand on the back of hers. She smiled and flipped her hand over, gripping him palm to palm across the table. And finally, the choke-hold on her words released.

"Thank you, Stephen," she said. "I don't know why you're here, but I will be forever grateful."

He brought her hand to his mouth and pressed a kiss into her palm. "When I realized that bastard had you…" His hand tightened.

"He didn't hurt me. It was just scary for a bit, that's all."

He exhaled, obviously getting a grip on his emotions. "It could have been a lot worse."

"But it wasn't. Thanks to you."

She pulled her hand away to tear a piece of her sticky bun off. But within a moment, she was reaching across the table. He more than met her halfway, and soon they were holding hands again across the booth.

"Why did you come back, Stephen?" she finally asked.

He searched her face, looking at her closely. "We can talk later. It's been a terrible day—"

"It's been awful, but, Stephen, I have to know now." She took a deep breath. "Why are you here?"

He searched her face, but must have been satisfied with whatever he saw. He gave her a smile and took a breath. Finally, she was going to have her answer.

"I quit my job."

Zoe blinked. That was not at all what she expected to hear. "What?"

"You were right. I don't belong in Hong Kong. I belong in Chong Ching."

Zoe gasped. "That's wonderful!" But then her

thoughts leaped ahead. "You came all the way from China to fire me?"

"No! No!" Then he frowned and ran a hand through his hair. He looked rumpled and distressed, but his eyes were intense as he focused on her face. "Ask me again why the Tigress Mother would not let us continue as partners."

She shook her head, struggling to keep up. "What?"

"Back in China, you asked me why. Why she would break us up as partners."

She remembered. "Okay. Why?"

"Because I am in love with you, Zoe. Because I have fallen in love and want…" He reached into his jacket pocket and pulled out a jeweler's box. He fumbled with it one-handed, but in the end he managed to flip it open. Inside, a tiny lightbulb flicked on to shine on a diamond ring.

"Oh, my God."

"I got all the way to the airport before I realized it wasn't the work in Chong Ching I desperately needed. I need you. Zoe, I know you wouldn't be the boss's mistress, but what about his wife? You will still be respected, and we could work together every day."

"Oh, my God."

"I love you, Zoe. Do you think—"

"Yes!" She couldn't believe it was true. She couldn't believe she was finally able to say it aloud! She'd been pretending she wasn't in love for so long now. Finally, she could let her heart open and all that love rush through. "I love you, too! I wanted to tell you, but I didn't think you…" Then she threw herself across the booth and into his arms.

It might have gone further, if the circumstances were different. If they weren't in a booth in a public café. But they were, so she contented herself with a kiss. A really long kiss. A really fabulously wonderful kiss.

And then she had to sit back because he was trying to take hold of her left hand. She was trembling, she realized, but so was he as he slipped the ring onto her finger.

"Oh, my God," she murmured for the third time as she looked at the beautiful diamond. But then she started talking, saying words without thought as she stared and stared at the ring on her finger. He loved her! He wanted to marry her! "I still intend to finish school."

"Of course!" he returned, sounding insulted that she would think anything different.

"And is there room in your company for me? Not the pork part. The incubator. I mean, I'd still like to—"

"There is more than enough work for two of us. Especially since I'd like to expand farther north of Chong Ching."

Zoe giggled. Trust Stephen to be thinking expansion already. But then his eyes turned serious.

"I want to work in China, Zoe. I want to continue everything I started in Chong Ching. But if you want to live in the United States, I would understand. I want to be with you, wherever you are. And I could start another incubator here if need be."

She shook her head with alarm. "No! No! There's so much more we could do there. Oh, Stephen, I want to be with you. I love you. I'll go anywhere—"

This time he was the one stretching across the booth to kiss her. She met him more than halfway, and once again, things would have gone differently if they weren't in public. But in the end, they eased apart.

There was so much to plan, so much to do, so many details to discuss. She saw the same awareness in his eyes, but neither one spoke. That was for later. Right now, they both were too busy just being with each other, holding hands and knowing they were in love. They loved each other!

"I'm starting to think it is possible," Zoe finally said.

"What?"

"A career, a man. Maybe even a family?"

His eyes shimmered as he nodded. "I would like that very much."

"So would I," she whispered. "Oh, yes, it is possible!" Then she laughed, the realization hitting her broadside. She could have it all: career, family and love. Most especially love. Not to mention the whole wide world in which to work. This was going to be great. Her whole life was going to be just *great!*

HARLEQUIN
60
YEARS
of pure reading pleasure

We'll be spotlighting a different series
every month throughout 2009
to celebrate our 60th anniversary.

Look for Silhouette® Nocturne™ in October!

Travel through time to experience tales
that reach the boundaries of life and death.
Bestselling authors Lindsay McKenna, Cindy
Dees, P.C. Cast and Merline Lovelace join
together in a brand-new, four-book
Time Raiders miniseries.

TIME RAIDERS

August—*The Seeker*
by *USA TODAY* bestselling author Lindsay McKenna

September—*The Slayer* by Cindy Dees

October—*The Avenger*
by *New York Times* bestselling author and
coauthor of the House of Night novels P.C. Cast

November—*The Protector*
by *USA TODAY* bestselling author Merline Lovelace

Available wherever books are sold.

nocturne™

New York Times bestselling author
and co-author of the House of Night novels

P.C. CAST

makes her stellar debut
in Silhouette® Nocturne™

THE AVENGER

Available October wherever books are sold.

SNBPA09R

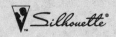

SPECIAL EDITION

FROM *NEW YORK TIMES* BESTSELLING AUTHOR

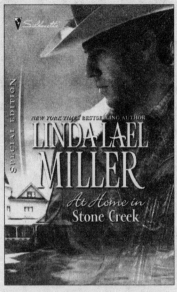

Ashley O'Ballivan had her heart broken by a man years
ago—and now he's mysteriously back. Jack McCall *isn't*
the person she thinks he is. For her sake, he must keep
his distance, but his feelings for her are powerful.
To protect her—from his enemies and himself—he
has to leave...vowing to fight his way home to
her and Stone Creek forever.

Available in November wherever books are sold.

Visit Silhouette Books at www.eHarlequin.com

You're invited to join our Tell Harlequin Reader Panel!

By joining our new reader panel you will:

- Receive Harlequin® books—they are FREE and yours to keep with no obligation to purchase anything!
- Participate in fun online surveys
- Exchange opinions and ideas with women just like you
- Have a say in our new book ideas and help us publish the best in women's fiction

In addition, you will have a chance to win great prizes and receive special gifts! See Web site for details. Some conditions apply. Space is limited.

To join, visit us at

www.TellHarlequin.com.

REQUEST YOUR FREE BOOKS!

2 FREE NOVELS PLUS 2 FREE GIFTS!

HARLEQUIN®

Blaze

Red-hot reads!

Stay up-to-date on all your romance reading news!

The Harlequin Inside Romance newsletter is a **FREE** quarterly newsletter highlighting our upcoming series releases and promotions!

Go to
eHarlequin.com/InsideRomance
or e-mail us at
InsideRomance@Harlequin.com
to sign up to receive
your **FREE** newsletter today!

COMING NEXT MONTH

Available September 29, 2009

#495 TOUCH ME Jacquie D'Alessandro
Historicals
After spending ten years as a nobleman's mistress, Genevieve Ralston's no stranger to good sex. So when she meets an irresistible stranger with seduction on his mind, she's game. Only little does she guess he wants much more than her body....

#495 CODY Kimberly Raye
Love at First Bite
All Miranda Rivers wants is a simple one-night stand. But when she picks up sexy rodeo star—and vampire—Cody Braddock, that one night might last an eternity....

#497 DANGEROUS CURVES Karen Anders
Undercover Lovers
Distract her rival agent, hot and handsome Max Carpenter, for two weeks—that's Rio Marshall's latest DEA assignment. But in the steamy Hawaiian hideaway, who'll be distracting whom?

#498 CAUGHT IN THE ACT Samantha Hunter
Dressed to Thrill
Wearing a bold 'n' sexy singer's costume has Gina Thomas delivering a standout performance that gives her the chance to search for scandalous photos of her sister. But it also captures the attention of Mason Scott—keeper of said photos. So what will he request when he catches Gina red-handed?

#499 RIPPED! Jennifer LaBrecque
Uniformly Hot!
Lieutenant Colonel Mitch Cooper is a play-by-the-rules kind of guy. Too bad his latest assignment is to keep an eye on free-spirited Eden Walters, who only wants to play...with him!

#500 SEDUCTION BY THE BOOK Stephanie Bond
Encounters
When four Southern wallflowers form a book club, they don't realize they're playing with fire. Because in *this* club, the members are reading classic erotic volumes, learning how to seduce the man of their dreams. After a book or two, Atlanta's male population won't stand a chance!

HBCNMBPA0909